My Life is the High Life

Gene Suttle

Other books by Gene Suttle

My Way is the High Way

Copyright © 2011 Gene Suttle

All rights reserved. No part of this publication may be reproduced, stored in a retrieval system, or transmitted in any form or by any means, electronic, mechanical, recording or otherwise, without the prior written permission of the author.

The characters and events in this book are fictitious. Any similarity to real persons, living or dead, is coincidental and not intended by the author. Shasta is a fictional town and Shasta High School is a fictional school. Texas is real as are several towns and places used fictitiously.

Second Edition

For my children

A man's got to take a lot of punishment to write a really funny book.
-Ernest Hemingway

Every saint has a past and every sinner has a future.
-Oscar Wilde

Another Monday

I.

"You big prick!" The words echoing off the back wall of the office indicated to me the lady on the opposite side of the counter was not happy. The flared nostrils, red face, and bony finger tapping on my chest convinced me.

I knew better. I'm a highly trained administrator and the best way to diffuse a situation is to listen and let the steam bleed off, but damn it, it was Monday morning, my head hurt, and it wasn't even 8:30 yet. Plus, it was just too good of an opening to pass up. She had thrown me a high looping curve ball that my grandmother could have knocked out of the park.

"Mrs. Fisher," I said calmly. "I know you have seen a lot of pricks and are probably an expert. I also appreciate your assessment of mine. It's not often women use the words big and prick around me at the same time, but you have and I'm grateful. However, even with the flattery I still can't excuse little Layton's absence."

I had never seen the shade of red Mrs. Fisher's face was turning. I think it fell somewhere between scarlet and crimson on the color wheel. She was gasping for air and I honestly thought she might have a seizure. Calling on my exceptional decision making skills and having assessed the situation, it appeared that my best course of action was to dismiss myself before she was able to regain her composure so I calmly walked back into my office and sat down. As I swallowed aspirins #7 and #8 since I woke up this morning, I heard the office door slam loud enough to break windows in the gym. I knew better. I also knew this wasn't over.

As the ringing continued in my ears from the yelling and slamming, I closed my eyes and rubbed my temples. When I opened them again a few seconds later, Ms. Shelly was standing in the doorway with her arms folded and a hint of smile on her face. It was hard to tell if she was happy, amused, or astonished. Having known Ms. Shelly now for twelve years and having had some very intimate personal experiences with her over that time, I was sure she was wondering if I was really that stupid or if I was having a seizure.

"You do know that Abigail Fisher is Super Dan's niece right?" Ms. Shelly asked in the calmest voice. She already knew the answer, but was making a point. Super Dan was the superintendent, former championship football coach, and had had lived in Shasta for sixty plus years, the last thirty in the superintendent's office.

"Yes ma'am, I am aware of that connection." I responded, not making eye contact. "There are just some times when enough is enough and I guess I didn't have any political correctness left this morning, Ms. Shelly. " I explained very lamely.

"Do you have leads on a new job I don't know about?" sarcasm dripped from every word. See, Ms. Shelly and I had this discussion last fall when I was almost fired over the cheerleader car wash down on Main Street. The fact they wore their bikinis and used some suggestive advertisement to drum up business was bad, but they did it on a Sunday afternoon right after church. In this town, that was as close to Satan coming to visit as anyone could imagine. As principal of Shasta High School, most everyone felt I should have been the one sacrificed on the altar to atone for the sins of this school and spare the town from certain destruction. Fortunately, with a little luck and some blackmail, I had saved my job, but had been given a clear warning. Not by the board or the Superintendent, but by Ms. Shelly who had had more than her share of losers cross her path. She had encouraged me to grow up and start acting my age and get rid of some of the self-destructive behaviors I seemed to cling to. I cared about a lot of things, but nothing compared to the way I cared about Ms. Shelly so I had really cleaned up my act…. up until about five minutes ago. Then I fell off the wagon.

"I'm going to walk down the hall and I'll be back in a minute. When Super Dan calls tell him I'm dealing with something or other and I'll get back to him shortly. I'll figure something out by then, okay?" I ask as a question, but mostly was talking to myself since I was the one that needed convincing.

As I walked by, Ms. Shelly touched my hand in and said, "I know you try hard, but at times you just have to be you. There's just no way around it. And to be honest, Mrs. Fisher didn't give you much of a choice. If you must know, I giggled behind the folder I had in my hand. That was quite funny. I guess I'm just drawn to the unruly ones, the bad boys. It must be my fate and I need to learn to live with it." She finished with a wink and a smile, which made me feel a whole lot better than I did a few minutes ago.

II.

My name is William Robert Masters and I've been the principal of Shasta High School for the last twelve years. My parents had named me for dignity and success, but society had decided Billy Bob suited me better so I answer to any and all variations. Bill and Billy prevailed among my friends and as you have seen my detractors used many other names including prick.

Shasta was a small town about an hour outside Fort Worth and about two hours south of Oklahoma City. Our closest Wal-Mart was in Decatur, but no true Shasta citizen would step foot in that store so we had to travel to Wichita Falls to get discounted groceries or buy our necessities down at Mayfield's on Main street. It seemed Shasta and Decatur both made bids for the Wal-Mart store and rumor had it that Decatur stole the store with a last-minute cash offering made to the selection committee under the table. The official press release from Bentonville, Arkansas identified the location right on a major highway as the key deciding factor, but nobody in Shasta believed it.

Dan Cochran, the superintendent, commonly known as Super Dan, had hired me away from a high school in the panhandle of Texas to come in and raise the level of achievement and bring Shasta High School up to a standard that the town could be proud of. Every state education indicator would show that had been accomplished beyond expectation, however the folks in Shasta had their own measuring stick and a few still felt like I didn't measure up.

My first problem was my hair, which was a little longer than they liked around here. Of course anything longer than a buzz cut would fall into that category. I also had an attitude problem, my attitude was seen as too liberal, and I gave the students way too much latitude at school. Considering the conservative nature of the townsfolk that had lived here for generations, the only way I could have measured up would have been to run the school more like a reformatory with uniforms and formations. That, in my opinion, was archaic and I said so many times. The words 'liberal damn hippie' was used so often that that's the only way many of the citizens knew me. So it's not surprising that a few times each year I had been called to task in front of the board about one issue or other in hopes that the board would run me off. I guess my greatest accomplishment was that I still had a job after twelve years. I do have to admit that last fall I thought my streak had run out, but I survived...until today.

Ms. Shelly was right, Mrs. Fisher was Super Dan's niece, she was in fact the daughter of his wife, Thelma's baby sister and that's trouble. Ms. Shelly of course was always right and was why I was glad to have her in the office. That, and the fact she smelled good, felt good, and came over to my house every Thursday night for supper and an occasional baring of our souls and bodies. The first person I hired when I got to Shasta was Ms. Shelly who was a single mother of two needing a job to pay back some debts run up by a former lowlife husband. We hit it off right away. We made a great team at work, but over time we had developed a personal relationship that would be the closest thing to marriage if we had actually lived together, which we didn't.

Friends with benefits would be too cheap and shallow as a descriptor. We were lovers, both of whom had gone through two failed marriages, that wanted someone in our lives, but weren't quite ready to pull the trigger again. My marital problems were the result of spending way too much time away from home so that my exes had to find other ways to entertain themselves. Ms. Shelly had a heart for lost causes and stray animals. She was one of those that had too kind of heart and always wound up with the worst possible men. I was thinking that's how I had managed to make my way into her heart. She saw a lost cause and thought she could save me. I had to admit, she'd done a hell of a job so far. I just didn't want to hurt her like the rest had. So far it had been the right fit for both of us, but I knew it came down to me. She was mine to have, if I didn't screw it up.

III.

When I walked out of the office door, I had no particular place to go. I had thought about walking around the building for a while or maybe out to the field house. Mainly, I needed a few minutes to figure out how to handle Super Dan when he called. I knew he would have no wiggle room whatsoever with Thelma squeezing his balls until I screamed.

I really was a good principal and over the last twenty years had led three campuses to outstanding achievement by following the basic principles of leadership I had adopted. I called them the 3 N's-Instinct, Energy, and Enthusiasm. Now, I had read the books and been to the trainings, but when the rubber met the road, when a principal was in the trenches making decisions at a rapid fire pace, there wasn't time for any of that group decision making stuff everyone was so proud of and state educators touted as the way to go. That's bullshit. I had never once seen a group decision-making team standing beside me in front of the board when I was getting a butt chewing. I never expected they would.

That's why when decisions needed to be made, I made them and if shit hit the fan, well I made the mess and I would clean it up. As far as group decision-making, I had it on my campus. I wrote up the report and the group got to decide if they wanted to sign it or not. No one complained because I took good care of my teachers and they would only turn on me if it came down to their jobs so it was important to keep the faculty happy.

My instincts were good and were backed up by being in constant motion, and being excited about my job, my school, and being around the kids. When I fully utilized all these skills, things went well, except…. Have you ever seen a railroad crossing that had the crossing arms with flashing lights that came down when a train was coming? Have you ever seen someone dash around the arms ahead of the train because they're in too big a hurry to stop? Have you ever heard of someone getting run over doing that? Failing to heed the warning signs and getting smashed. When I got into trouble was when my instincts threw up the crossing arms, flashing lights, and warnings…. and yet I barreled right on through. This morning was like that. I knew who I was dealing with. My gut said just excuse the kid's absence and let it go, but self-destructive behavior reared its head in my life occasionally according to Ms. Shelly. I seemed to have a death wish or a desire to tempt fate. Either way was not good. So here I am. I need to fix this one and fast. After giving it a little thought, what better place to think than in the gym watching Coach Connelly's volleyball workout? So I turned around and headed to the gym.

IV.

When I looked in the gym, I was surprised to see a large number of guys when I had expected to see the volleyball girls going through off season drills or something. Curious, I stepped inside and saw Debbie Connelly by the far wall chatting with a few girls while the guys clustered around the bleachers on the south side. It appeared more like a before school chat time than first period off-season volleyball. When Debbie saw me she smiled and began to make her way across the gym. This of course was one of the reasons I liked to come to the gym - to watch as her long legs moved. It was quite the site.

Debbie was in her second year as head girls coach at Shasta High after starring on the University of Nebraska's championship volleyball team for three years. Looking at her head full of red hair that curled and flew in all directions as well as the freckles that were sprinkled around her face and neck made me start humming *Irish Eyes are Smiling* subconsciously every time she came into view. The crazy thing was that if you closed your eyes and only heard her talk you would picture Mint Juleps, Southern Mansions, and parasols. Being from the South, she had a voice as smooth and syrupy as warm molasses.

I had taken it upon myself to mentor Debbie when she first arrived and that mostly meant chatting her up every chance I got. She was good-natured about it and the flirting was mostly for my benefit and ego. She laughed at the right times and gave back as good as I dished out. In the back of my mind of course, I imagined another scenario, but was smart enough to realize that innocent flirting would be the extent of our involvement, but a guy could dream right?

"Hey Debbie,'" I said as she walked up beside me and playfully punched me on the shoulder. It was a little intimidating to talk face to chest with a woman, which I had to do when Debbie wore her three-inch heels. With her chest, I figured I would suck it up and take one for the team. Normally she had on tennis shoes and I could stand up straight and at least be close to the same height, but she was all dressed up for a Monday with no game on the schedule. "Wow, don't you look good this morning? Is that a new outfit? I guess I didn't realize we had a game somewhere today. Surely you aren't wearing that to a softball game."

"No silly, there's no game. I just thought I would actually wear clothes to school today instead of warm ups," she said as she did a model twirl and displayed a dress that clung to all the right spots and accented her fiery red hair.

"Hmmmmm Hmmmmm Hmmm Hmmm Hm," was all that came out of my mouth as my brain locked up with an overload of emotions and signals it was getting and sending out. Total shutdown.

Debbie smiled at the effect she had and said, "I take it that you approve? Should I dress up more often?"

Finally regaining control of my tongue I was able to respond, "As nice as that would be, I am afraid it would cause complete chaos at the school and we would get nothing done. As you can see half of the male population of this school is already down here in the gym instead of being in class on a Monday morning. It would be that way everyday. I assume they all heard about your dress. "

Turning to look towards the other end of the gym she laughed and said, "Billy, those boys aren't here for me. They came to see Demarcus."

"Demarcus?" I asked. I didn't remember having any student or faculty by that name.

"Demarcus Latham. The football player? All-American at Nebraska? NFL Rookie of the Year for Tampa Bay?" she kept giving me hints until I nodded I recognized the name.

"So Demarcus Latham is in our gym?" I asked still unsure what she was telling me.

""Yea, he's right down there talking to the guys and signing autographs," she responded smiling a different kind of smile this time.

"Is this some sort of outreach program you set up and I knew about that slipped my mind?" I asked confused by the whole setting.

"Oh no!" She laughed. "Demarcus is here to see me and I thought the kids would get a kick out of seeing him. He came to take me to dinner." She added with a very unassuming air.

"So you know Demarcus? You two know each other well enough to go out to dinner?" I asked starting to put the pieces together, but still not sure where it was going.

"Billy! Demarcus is my fiancé. He and I have been dating since we were freshmen at Nebraska. He proposed last year on the night he was drafted. We are going to get married in June. I will want you to be there okay?" She had taken both my hands and was jumping up in down in three inch heels excited as a schoolgirl. Normally, with a face full of bouncing breast, I would have only one train of thought, but what she had just said overrode even those emotions.

"Wait!" I said with a little more urgency than was required. "Does he know we are lovers?" I asked, hoping to conjure up a reason for her not to marry this guy. I knew if she did he'd probably want her to move to where the hell ever he had some 15,000 square foot mansion built, probably on a beach with an infinity pool off the patio. Damn Damn Damn.

"I would say that you stopping by the gym to look at my legs and make suggestive comments would hardly qualify us as lovers!" she laughed and brushed it off with the flip of her long red hair.

Feigning deep hurt and feeling some real hurt, I said, "I guess maybe you haven' taken this relation quite as serious as I have. That's really disappointing to find out now after having invested two years of my life with you."

"Billy, you know I will always love you, but Demarcus is the one I'm going to marry and it's probably best he doesn't hear you say anything about being lovers even if you are joking. He's pretty big and very jealous!" she warned.

14

"So all this time we've spent together you've simply seen as folly? A way to get your entertainment and then you toss me aside for the first bum that comes along with a fast car and a big diamond?" I was rolling now. I hadn't played this much drama since high school.

She was laughing full force and thought my act was great. Unfortunately, it wasn't all an act. I was so convincing because I did care a lot about Coach Connelly and would miss her when she was gone and if she married Demarcus she'd be gone soon.

"Come on, I'll introduce you. I've talked a lot about you and he wanted to meet you." She said as she took one hand leading me across the gym.

"You've talked about me, but you didn't mention we were lovers? What did you say? What does he know and do I want to get close to him?" All these questions by me were asked as we walked closer to the crowd of boys.

"I told him you have been like a father figure to me. Someone that's looked after me and made sure I was taken care of." She said softly and with a smile. "He really appreciates that, by the way."

"Father figure? Oh jeez. Father figure? Oh crap. Seriously? Father figure? Couldn't you have said crazy uncle or something like that? The guy at reunions that everyone laughs at even when he pinches the ladies butts and talks dirty?" I asked pleadingly. "Father figure means I have to go erase all those beach volleyball tournaments of yours I have taped and then wash my mind out with soap!"

She stopped halfway across the gym and this time she spoke softly, "Look, I have appreciated all you have done for me and you have been a great friend these past two years. I am so glad you have Ms. Shelly because y'all make a great couple." At that my eyes must have widened, because she added, "Yes, I know you've been cheating on me," she winked as she said it. "And so does everyone else that lives in this town and is still breathing. It's not like we can't see it when you two look at each other. Don't worry, everyone thinks its great and only wonders why you haven't already gotten married."

I could tell this was important to her and she didn't need any of my adolescent bullshit. It was time to quit playing games and to be mature about the whole thing. I was going to miss her, but I looked at her and smiled and with all sincerity I congratulated her on her upcoming wedding. Then I made her promise to invite Ms. Shelly and me. We then pushed our way through the guys clustered around Demarcus.

"Hey Demarcus!" Debbie yelled, "I have someone for you to meet."

As he rose from his seat I had time to be grateful several times that he saw me as Debbie's father and not her lover. He had to be the biggest man I had ever seen and by the time he stood up straight he blocked out most of the light on one end of the gym. He reached out a hand that head-slapped offensive tackles as he rushed past them to crush quarterbacks into the ground. As his hand enveloped mine, I swear his fingers overlapped his thumb so he could grip my hand.

"Demarcus, this is William Robert Masterson, my principal. We call him Billy usually though. Billy, Demarcus Latham, my fiancé," Debbie did the introductions with class and pride all the way around.

"Billy, I can't tell you how nice it is to meet you. Debbie has told me so much about you and how you helped her get her program started here and all. Thank you for looking after her." His voice was a very low bass that sounded confident and at ease. He also was very sincere which made me feel kind of like a creep for some of the impure thoughts I had over the past couple years about his fiancé. Since I had been promoted to father figure there was not any chance those would be happening again that was for sure for all my shortcomings, pervert is not one of them.

"Demarcus! It's an honor to have you here at Shasta High. Wow, who would have thought? I know you made these guys day. You're getting a great gal in Debbie and I hope you two have a very happy life together. " I said with honesty and sincerity this time.

After a few more minutes of pleasantries and a warning to the guys to at least check in with their first period teachers before

16

the bell rang, I slipped back into the hall. It occurred to me I was in the gym because I had a problem and was supposed to be finding a solution. Finding out Debbie had a boyfriend was a surprise. Finding out her boyfriend was Demarcus Latham and they were getting married had stunned me like a Taser. I needed a way to clear my head and refocus so I walked towards the auditorium where it was dark and quiet. Many days I sat in the middle of the seats and pondered a lot of things as kids snuck across stage or giggled behind the curtain never knowing I was lurking in the dark.

V.

My radio crackled, as I was halfway between the gym and the auditorium. It was Boomer. Corliss Prescott Skinner, or Boomer as most people knew him, had worked as my assistant principal for the last twelve years. I had called him as soon as I arrived in Shasta and talked him into leaving his coaching job at a small school in West Texas so he could learn how to be an administrator. It didn't take a lot of talking and he had been dedicated and loyal to me ever since. Boomer's number one qualification for the job was his size; he was 6'7" and weighed in excess of 300 pounds. He had been an all world athlete in a little 1-A school north of Lubbock and had garnered a scholarship to Texas A&M, which is saying a lot for a kid from a high school that carried the entire graduating class to the South Plains Fair in a twelve passenger van. Unfortunately, Boomers SATs had not been very good and he wound up at a junior college and managed to get hurt before he ever had a chance to play in front of the Twelfth Man. Boomer didn't quit though. After transferring to Texas Tech, he focused on his classes until he graduated with a degree in History and set out to become an athletic director. I intervened and helped him refocus on the academic side of education that actually could help more in the long run than X's and O's. He never has regretted the change and will make a good principal one of these days. Right now he had a problem since he was using the radio.

"Hey, Boss." Boomer called. "You there?"

"Yeah, Boomer, go ahead. What do you have?" I asked never really knowing what Boomer is going to come up with.

"Boss, it seems we have a large number of students absent this morning even though they have been seen before school. I have teachers calling in from all over the building." He reported. "I think we may have a senior skip day in progress."

"Hey Boomer, are most of these students boys? If so they are all in the gym with Demarcus Latham. Coach Connelly put together a program and I forgot to get the list out. Let the teachers know they will all be back in class by the end of first period and send a note to Coach Connelly to run them out in time to check in." I lied just a little. Mainly it was to cover the guy's butts because I would have wanted to see Demarcus as well. Counting them absent wouldn't do anyone any good and we forget to put out excuse lists all the time. This time I can be the one to forget. As long as they are in the building we need to get credit for them and I figured they were enjoying this morning's lesson a lot more than the one scheduled in their classes. High school is about educating in many different ways for many different reasons. In a month, the seniors are going to be leaving for college, going to work, or maybe to war. There is plenty of time to be serious. I planned on getting serious pretty soon myself.

I opened the large door to the auditorium and slipped into the darkness. I stood inside the door long enough for my eyes to adjust and decided to slip into the back row and ponder my next move with Super Dan. I knew he had already called the office and I knew Ms. Shelly had been convincing about my whereabouts and desire to return his call as soon as I was free. I just needed to be free pretty soon and have all my ducks in a row. Super Dan hadn't been the worst boss I'd had and he really didn't have anything against me personally. I think he might actually have liked the way I got things done without bothering him with every little detail. The problem started when I had pissed off Coach Elmira Johnson my first year at Shasta High. She was old school and since she had been at it over thirty years at that time, her old school was one room schoolhouse old. I have since learned that she and Thelma Cochran have been friends since they were first year teachers and their classrooms were side by side. I suspect that was back when they also brought coal oil to keep their lanterns burning. So long story short, I crossed Elmira, Thelma's her best friend, Thelma's married to Super Dan, and for twelve years Thelma had done everything she could think of to make my life miserable. Most often that meant making Super Dan's life miserable first, which is why he usually was in a bad mood when he called. Take Thelma out of the picture and hell we might even go fishing together. Maybe.

As I sat in silence and let my mind wander searching for an answer, I heard faint breathing coming from behind me inside the sound booth. It had a regular pattern to it and seemed to increase in rhythm and intensity as I listened. I had heard that kind of breathing before and it usually involved a naked woman. I just shook my head and smiled in the dark as I walked quietly to the end of the row and slipped out the door and around to the sound booth entrance. The whole time I'm thinking, at least somebody's having a good Monday morning, I just wasn't sure who it was going to be.

I slowly turned the knob as quietly as I could and slid the door open. As light poured in illuminating the booth, I heard two gasps that coincided with the cries of ecstasy associated with their current behavior and sounded like both people almost hemorrhaged as the conflicting emotions collided in their chest. Both sets of eyes were glued to mine with fixed expressions of horror locked in place. I looked long enough to confirm that sex was actually taking place and told them to put their clothes back on and get themselves in order as I stood outside the door. Joe Bob Gordon and Chastity Wheeler. Chastity. Parents hoping for a child to live up to their name would soon be disappointed.

Of all the people I would have guessed, Joe Bob and Chastity would be the last and next to last on my list. Both were seniors, both spent most of their time with the theater arts teacher, and one act play when not singing in the choir. They were artistic people and both would be considered slightly obese. Now that's not to say that artistic people or obese people don't or shouldn't enjoy sex as much as anyone, but neither had ever been seen with a member of the opposite sex in public as far as I knew. But it appeared they had managed to find each other and spent at least one morning together. I guess we were fixing to find out.

Joe Bob came out first and was in full-scale panic. His face was red from either the exertion of the past few minutes or from hyperventilating the last few seconds. I was wondering if I needed to call the nurse. I motioned for him to stand against the wall while I assured him we were going to work this out and he needed to relax. He didn't seem to believe me on either count. Chastity made her appearance a few minutes later and I had to stifle a laugh as she came out with her blouse inside out. She too, was flushed and wide eyed.

"Chastity, honey. Just relax there, okay. I need you to slip back in there and flip you shirt right side out, can you do that?" I asked feeling almost sorry for having caused them so much grief.

A sob escaped from her mouth as she looked down in horror and quickly retreated back into the sound booth. Jim Bob had managed to regulate his breathing enough that I felt his life was no longer in danger. When Chastity returned with everything buttoned and pressed down, I had them both stand against wall where they chose to focus on their shoes.

"Okay. We have a problem we need to fix and I'm going to need some cooperation." I said fairly sternly, but with a lot of fatigue and resignation mixed in. "Who wants to tell me what you were thinking and how often this happens?"
Silence. Shuffling. Shoe staring.

"Joe Bob, you're the man. You chose to act like a man a few minutes ago and you need to act like the man now. Look up here and tell me what the hell you were thinking!" I verbally goosed him hoping to get something going so we could move on.

"Uh... well... uh... we thought we would screw ... uh ... in the sound booth since ... uh ... no one was around. It was dark and quiet." He said as if that was a revelation to me.

"I get that you two were screwing. I believe we can stipulate that from now on, what I need to know is why you chose here at school so I have to get involved with your sex life for gosh sake!" I was starting to get a little frustrated with this Monday morning.

"Well sir... uh... its like this... uh.... We didn't really have anywhere else to do it." He said once again as if that made it understandable.

Now I stood silent, stymied by such honesty and really not sure what to say next. "Okay, I understand that this was a good place, it was quiet and dark, and private. I understand. All that makes for a good place to have sex. I agree. If I were going to have sex at school, I probably would pick the sound booth as well. So here's the question...who says you have to have sex at school or sex at all for that matter?" Once again my voice began to rise with frustration.

"Mr. Masters," Chastity spoke for the first time. "I think maybe I can help clarify a little if I may. "

"Chastity, sweetheart, if you can clarify, you most certainly may, because Joe Bob and I here aren't making any headway." I smiled as I turned toward her and gave her my full attention.

"You see Joe Bob and I have been seeing each other for the last two years. We've kept it fairly secret since our parents really aren't in favor of our dating. I don't know if you have ever heard of the Gordon-Wheeler feud, but its been going on for several generations in and around Shasta. It has something to do with mineral rights and land between our two families and that has led to several shootings and at least one hanging. Nobody today really understands it, but Wheelers aren't supposed to have anything to do with a Gordon, but we really love each other!" She explained patiently as a teacher would to a slow learner.

I nodded my head that I was following her and said, "Okay guys, I'm all for the Romeo Juliet thing, I get you love each other, and I really appreciate the fact that there are soul mates out there for each of us. I'm glad you two were able to find yours at such an early age. I don't think any of us have a problem with that. One more time though, Chastity, why is necessary for you to have sex here at school, which is a problem for me?" I asked patiently hoping to try a new tactic.

"Mr. Masters, can we trust you?" she asked.

"Sure. I'm really not trying to get anyone in trouble or shot for sure," I said.

Chastity paused as she looked at Joe Bob who nodded his head in agreement to whatever question she had silently asked, "We got married two weeks ago and haven't even had a honeymoon yet. We thought we could make it until we graduate in a few weeks then we planned to go off to college and never let our families know or come back here. We just have been so frustrated that we took a chance to consummate our marriage in the sound booth!"

I'm sure my mouth was open as I stared at each of them in turn. I took a minute to compose myself and looked at their faces. They were both happy and fearful at the same time. Someone knew their secret, a secret that could cause painful consequences were the wrong people to find out.

"Guys, your telling me you're married and have been for two weeks?" I asked and they both nodded their heads. "You wouldn't bullshit me about this would you, because we all sink in that case. " This time they nodded no. "And you haven't even had a honeymoon?" Once again no. "So do you live at your own houses and just see each other at school?" Both heads bobbed up and down. "Jeez looweeze!"

I pulled out my wallet and found a handful of twenties. I held them out to Joe Bob and said, "Both of you go home this afternoon and tell your folks you have been selected as the Shasta High Ambassadors to the state convention for youth leaders. The convention is being held in Fort Worth and it last three days. You will be staying in a hotel and you leave tomorrow. Okay? Do you guys have a car?" Joe Bob said he did. "Good then both of you come tomorrow with a suitcase and leave from here. Joe Bob, bring the car and I will make you reservations in a hotel in Fort Worth. This money is for eating or drinking, which ever you choose. Everyone deserves a honeymoon." Both were starting to relax and smile at this point so I added with emphasis, "We both have a lot to lose if this gets out, understood?"

"We understand and thank you, Mr. Masters. We won't forget this!" Chastity said as she jumped up and hugged my neck. They scurried off back into the theater arts room as if they were afraid I would change my mind.

I looked at the clock and it wasn't even 9:30. I seriously wondered if I would survive this day. Odds were definitely stacking up against me. I took a deep breath and headed back to the office. I didn't have a solution, but it was time to face the music.

VI.

I got to the office just as the bell rang to dismiss first period. I stood in the hall long enough to see that an orderly procession began up and down the hall towards second period classes. I was hoping all the guys made it to first period and I would have to write up a school activity list for those that had chosen to risk an absence to see the Rookie of the Year in the NFL. Tardys this time of year were very expensive and sometimes caused students to lose their exemptions. Me? I wanted all the students to be exempt. The fewer we had testing the last few days, the more time I could spend getting ready for graduation.

I figured this "program" we had in the gym this morning would be classified as career planning or something along those lines. I am sure each young man is different in a positive way for having had the chance to interact with a highly trained professional. Anyway, they would all be excused and the Texas Education Agency could ask me to explain it if they wanted too. I am very good when it comes to political correctness and smoke screens. I have the natural gift of bullshit and I've also had a lot of practice. I never jeopardize a kid's future, but I do bend some of the rules created by non-educators for what they feel is the good of the students and I happen to disagree. Since they didn't ask my opinion when they made the rules, I really don't feel like I need to consult them when I interpret the rules. School was about kids and learning. That always happened, I guarantee.

As the halls began to clear, I pushed through the door to the office and headed around behind the counter. I saw the pink phone message taped to my doorframe and looked at Ms. Shelly long enough for her to nod indicating that Super Dan had indeed called. I grabbed the note as I walked by and read it as I plopped down in my chair. It seemed I had an 11:00 meeting with the superintendent in his office. There was no indication that he wanted to know if that suited my calendar or if I needed it to be at another more convenient time. I smiled at the thought of him asking anything. I guess I had about an hour to take care of some paper work before driving over to Central.

I picked up the phone and called the Hilton Express off the freeway down in Fort Worth and made reservations for Joe Bob and Chastity Gordon for three nights and prepaid with my Visa. I wrote down the conformation number on a piece of paper, sealed it in an envelope with directions, and had an office aide to courier it to Chastity in her second period classroom. She seemed a little more in control and focused than Joe Bob, but I had to give him credit, he had found him a good woman and I hoped he took care of her. They had some challenges ahead, but both being honor students they'd figure it out. I also wrote up an excuse list for attendance concerning Joe Bob and Chastity being our ambassadors to the leadership conference the next three days so they wouldn't be counted absent. That along with the list that excused all the guys this morning went out together.

"Hey, Boss?" Boomer's voice came over the radio just as I was loading up my briefcase with papers that need to go with me to Central office.

"Yeah Boomer?" I asked, once again crossing my fingers that something else hadn't blown up this morning. If so he was going to have to handle it.

"I'm down here in the cafeteria and they're having chili cheese dogs for lunch. Do you want me to bring you a couple?" Boomer sounded as if he had at least one of them stuffed in his mouth right now and it wasn't 10:30 yet.

"Boom, it's a little early for me so if you want, you can have my two. I have got to meet with Super Dan at 11:00 and it could be a while. Can you handle lunch by yourself if I'm not back?" I asked knowing full well Boomer could handle anything short of a terrorist t attack.

"No problem, Boss. Hey and thanks for the dogs. I had gone ahead and gotten them so I'll make sure they're eaten." Boomer signed off, but not before I heard another large bite being shoved into his mouth. Just thinking about chili cheese dogs today made me queasy, but for breakfast it was almost too much.

I breezed by Ms. Shelly's desk long enough to place my hand on the middle of her back and lean close enough to smell her perfume. Her smell worked liked amphetamines for me. It started my heart racing and definitely raised my blood pressure. With new energy and purpose, I told her I had a meeting loud enough for those around to hear me talking business and that I would be back when the meeting ended…. hopefully, I added much quieter. She smiled and said she'd make a note and off I went.

VII.

Gladys Newman was on the phone when I arrived at Super Dan's office. Gladys had been his secretary for the entire thirty years he had been superintendent and I believe they may have gone back even to when he was athletic director. They had grown to look eerily alike as much as a man and woman could. Over time it appeared they had acquired the same disposition as well or maybe they were already alike and that is why they stayed together so long. Chicken or the egg argument. I was mulling this over for the hundredth time when Gladys cocked her head and indicated for me to sit in one of the chairs. Super Dan's door was closed and I didn't know if he was gone or in another meeting. Gladys, I doubted, would be telling me so I sat down and thumbed through one of the out of date periodicals that lay on the table. I had flash backs to a doctor's waiting room feeling the same nervous anticipation and concern as to the outcome.

After a brief conversation over the phone in which I managed to only hear a few muffled words, I got the impression she had reported to the person on the other end that I was sitting in the office now. If I was a betting man, and I am, I would go all in on Thelma being the person on the other end of the line. Gladys was more loyal to Thelma than Dan and I imagine she kept Thelma in the loop on everything. Once again I suspect they both were about to wet their pants at the thought of my impending doom. Whatever happened I wouldn't give either one of them the satisfaction of seeing me cry or beg. I'd save that for the darkness of my house and probably when I'm talking to God about how I'm going to get out of this mess. I took a deep breath and decided not to get too far ahead of myself and worry about things that hadn't happened yet.

In a few minutes Super Dan's office door opened and he motioned me in. No one was inside so I had to guess he was either on the phone, checking e-mail, or having a morning nap. All of which was possible. I took the seat on the left in front of his desk as he closed the door and walked back around to sit down. From behind his desk he looked at me with arms folded, leaning back to the outer limits of his chair, with something between a smirk and smile on his face. Finally he said, "Billy, damn it, I want to like you and I really try, but just about the time I think everything's going to be all right, you go and get my ass in a bind all over again. It seems I've spent half my life getting my ass chewed out by Thelma, because you have upset her about one thing or another. She wants me to fire your ass and get you gone!"

He had paused, but I knew he wasn't through so I just nodded solemnly as if I agreed with him and his assessment of me as being a dumbass.

"Now Billy, last fall I seriously thought you had finally gone and done it with that gawd awful carwash business and those cheerleaders, but for some odd reason the board decided to back you and let you keep working here. To this day I'm not sure how that happened, but you got a new lease on life. Since then you've kept your nose clean and I was actually beginning to think we had passed on over to a new level of professionalism...until I get the call this morning. A whore? Seriously, you call Thelma's niece a whore right in the main office and expect me to be able to protect you!"

At that, I sat up waving my hands as if signaling a time out. "Dan, I know I do things differently than some folks want and I will never be able to please Thelma, but you've got to believe even I'm not stupid enough to call her niece a whore in public!" I said with as much sincerity as I could muster. "There were several witnesses that will back me on that, and if you want, I can take you through the entire incident."

Super Dan sat mulling this over for a few minutes. On one occasion, I honestly think he drifted off to another train of

26

thought and from his expression, it appeared much more pleasant then the one he was dealing with right now. I wonder what or who he was thinking of.

Finally he said, "In the interest of fairness let's hear your side of the story. I have heard Abigail's story from Thelma and it could have lost something in translation. I do know my wife despises you, but have never really understood why. She or Abigail may have embellished just a little. "

His sense of fairness and willingness to listen caught me off guard. He usually was just irritated and wanted me to do whatever was necessary to get rid of his aggravation.

"Abigail Fisher's son Layton, your great nephew, was absent last Friday and she came in this morning to have me give him an excuse so he could keep his test exemptions. I told her I was not able to that because the reason wasn't acceptable. She had already hammered Ms. Shelly unmercifully by the time I made it back from the cafeteria and you know how good Ms Shelly is about working with people and talking them down. By the time I intervened Abigail was wound tighter than catgut on a tennis racket. I listened to her story several times and each time I gave her the acceptable excuses and showed her why hers didn't work. She became frustrated and called me a prick. At that point is where I have to tell you, I messed up. I did infer that she might be an expert on pricks and I thanked her for her positive evaluation of mine. That of course is when she blew. Dan, I do apologize for my comments, but she was out of control and I had done all I could."

Now it was time I caught him off guard. I am sure he was trying to think if I had ever apologized before or admitted wrongdoing. It was something that had just come to me as the best strategy, which was to just tell the truth and admit my mistake. What a novel idea. It was his turn to sit and nod. We looked at each other for at least two minutes before he spoke again.

"What was little Layton doing last Friday that he needed to miss school?" Dan asked as a way to try and solve this.

"If I understand it correctly, little Layton wants to be a fashion designer and had gone to a taping of Project Runway over in

Dallas. Abigail felt like this should be seen as career exploration and wanted us to give him a college day." I related with a fairly even tone.

Dan's eyebrows rose with the mention of fashion design and red began to creep across his face as I finished.

"That kid has been weird his whole life. I gave him a football for Christmas one year when he was little and he cried. I knew right then he was going to be different. Fashion design. Are you kidding me? And Abigail is supporting this? That's what happens when there's not a man around the house to set an example by teaching the kid how to use power tools and watch the game on Saturday afternoon. He needs a father to have a catch out in the back yard before grilling steaks. Geez!"

Dan could have gone on and on using manly activities the kid needed to do, but I interrupted by asking if his father wasn't actually at home. Dan admitted he did have a father, but added the guy ran a florist shop for Christ sake. What kind of example was that? Spending all his time arranging flowers instead of being at home teaching his kid how to box or something. Of course, he said, even if it was flowers he couldn't blame him, Dan added as an after thought, since he wouldn't want to go home to Abigail either. She apparently was a miniature version of Thelma and Dan said himself that would make any man want to work late or travel often, which was his tactic.

So I sat there and waited as Dan lost himself in thought once again and I swear he left our conversation for a much more pleasurable place in his mind. I wondered if he was practicing Yoga or something. Maybe someone was teaching him how to center himself. Whatever he was doing was definitely working. When he came back to my reality, he seemed almost passive.

"Look Billy, I think you're a good guy and do your job well. I know every man has his limits and Thelma and Abigail can find those limits quicker than any two people I know. But here's the deal, I need you to give me something to take back to Thelma. She's not going to let this go and I need my life to get back to normal soon. What can we do here?"

Once again he went in a direction I didn't think he was capable of going. He actually asked for input and appeared to need my help. So I obliged. "Do you think if I call up Abigail and apologize for my behavior that that would do the trick?" I asked hopefully, because I can lie with a straight face if I had to. I could even sound sincere.

"That would be a starting point, but they are wanting blood. I may need to write you a reprimand and have Gladys put it in your file. She will make sure that Thelma knows what it says. I can take it out later. Can you live with that? Is there anyway we can change little Layton's absence? Is it really that big of deal?" He asked almost pleading.

"Dan, I would have excused it this morning had she not been so ugly to Ms. Shelly. Nobody abuses Ms. Shelly. I can change that to an excused absence and call it career development and to be honest, I just as soon he isn't there for semester test. Why don't you call Thelma and tell her you ate my ass out and wrote me up. Then you demanded an apology and for me to change his absence. I will call Abigail and offer my sincerest apology before the day is over. Will that fix this? I can do all that and not look back. Makes you look damn good in front of the family and I go back to my business. "

Dan smiled and thought for about a minute again. He didn't wander off this time so I know he was thinking how good he could make it sound to Thelma and maybe, just maybe, she would let him have his balls back for a while. He finally said, "I appreciate you not making this harder than it has to be and working with me. I wont forget. Oh, and hey, try to stay out of trouble for just a few more weeks, then we can all go fishing." This last part was added with a smile. I didn't know who this new Super Dan was, but I was starting to like him. I hope he hung around a while. Something told me Dan was getting laid and it wasn't by Thelma. A man's personality has a way of mellowing when there's regular loving involved. Now I just had to figure out who the lucky lady was.

VIII.

As I left Dan's office I tried to look cowed and beaten down like a man that had just had his head handed to him as I passed Gladys' desk. I knew she would be on the phone as soon as I

29

cleared the door filling Thelma in on the outcome. Helping sell the idea that Dan had ripped me a new one was important for me to get passed this and I dang sure did need to finish out the year without another incident. I probably had my quota this year of incidents and even my loyal supporters were probably getting weary.

I slid into to my truck and checked the time and was surprised to see it wasn't even noon yet. I would have sworn it had to be at least Thursday. As I slid my Merle Haggard's Greatest Hits into the CD player, *Mamma Tried* immediately reminded me that a lot of folks wanted me to be successful and the only thing holding me back was my own dumbass self. I really didn't want to go back to school just yet and I had faith Boomer could handle lunch, but to go to the Dairy Whiz would put me right in the middle of the dinner traffic. I was tired of answering questions about how our scores were going to turn out and how we were going to be rated. Honestly, with the Texas Education Agency changing the rules every stinking year, who the hell knew how the ratings were going to come out. I knew our kids were as smart as anyone's and I knew they tried as hard as anyone's because they knew it was important for us. They wanted to keep us around since we actually cared about what they thought and needed. If kids think you are straight with them, they always shot straight with you. That was a lesson I learned early on. The principals and superintendents that ignored the kids usually had short or unsuccessful careers.

I decided I might just drive out to the truck stop for lunch. They had a pretty good restaurant and few townspeople ate there. It was mostly the truckers and travelers that passed through. As I drove east, I called the school office on my cell.

"Shasta High School, Shelly speaking," Ms. Shelly said in her a very professional manner.

"Hey Shelly, Billy here. Just wanted you to know I was still standing and should be able to collect a paycheck for at least another month. " I said cheerfully and then added, "I'm going to grab a quick sandwich before I head back, can I bring you something?"

"Well that's good to know. I was wondering how it went. Are you okay?" she asked with legitimate concern.

"It was the strangest thing, I swear. I will tell you about when I get back, but Super Dan actually acted like a human. I really believe he's got himself a girlfriend somewhere. He was all about resolving this and working it out. Couldn't believe it. " I said trying to convince myself it was real. "Anyway, I'm good. How about lunch? You need anything?"

Shelly thought for a moment and then said, "I brought a salad. As much as I want a chicken fried steak, I had better stick with my sack lunch. I have book club tonight and we always have the best food. I also want to make sure I can fit into my swimsuit. Are we still going to the lake this weekend? First time of the summer you know, " She added with some extra excitement.

I had a place up at Palmer Lake just across the Red River into Oklahoma. We had gone each weekend we could get away from May until October for as long as I have had the place. It makes for a nice getaway and this weekend was the first time the water would be warm enough to float in. Just thinking about warm weather, cold beer, and the smell of suntan lotion kind of had me going. Ms. Shelly was all business at the office, but nobody had a better time at the lake than she did. She loved the outdoors and magical things happened when just enough waves and just enough beer and just enough sunshine were all mixed together. There's really nothing better than sex on a boat that's rocking to the rhythm of the waves and the beat of golden oldies rock and roll thumping out of speakers in the hull. Can you say *Good Vibrations*?

"Billy? Are you still there?" she asked.

Jolted back to reality, I smiled to myself and said, "Oh yeah Shelly, I was just imagining you and that little green swimsuit you wear so well. I had to pull over to get a hold of myself!"

"Hey focus on your business and I will see you back in the office shortly. " She ended the conversation by redirecting me back to reality and giving me a time limit for my lunch. All implied of course, but well understood.

The talk about lakes and thinking about suntan lotion called for some Jimmy Buffet so I changed out the CDs and listened to

It's Five o'clock Somewhere as I drove out to the truck stop on the edge of town. When I pulled into the parking lot, I complimented myself for such a good choice. There were a couple of eighteen-wheelers gassing up and a few more parked out back. I saw two cars on the curb, both with Oklahoma license plates, but didn't see one car that I could identify as someone that might want to engage me in a conversation. Yea for me. I might just enjoy this meal and Monday might be salvaged after all.

When I strolled in, the sign said seat myself so I opted for a booth by the window. I pulled out a greasy menu from behind the catsup and mustard bottles and scanned the fare. It seemed that the special for Monday was stew and cornbread. I had a feeling that meant cooking up all the weekend's leftovers into a nice soup. I decided to pass on that and was considering the enchiladas when Donna strolled up.

"Hey Mr. Masters, what can I get you to drink?" She asked

"Hey, Donna. I thought you worked the night shift. Are you on days now?" I asked, sincerely happy for her.

"No unfortunately, I'm pulling a double. One of the gals had to be in court this morning for a divorce hearing and I needed the money. Been here for fourteen hours and I'm about dead on my feet." She said as exhausted as she looked.

Donna and I went back a few years. She had graduated Shasta High before I arrived and immediately found herself the mother of two kiddos from two men that came and went. She was trying to make ends meet by working at the truck stop, which didn't pay all that well, but tips were good from the truckers. She had found that when times got really hard, she could crawl into the sleeper cabs and pick up some extra cash, but saved that as a last resort. Her daughter and I had come to an understanding a couple of years back when she wanted to rebel and I let her as long as she made her grades. She would be graduating this year and going on to college. Her son was a lazy piece of worthlessness until I came to his house and took his Xbox and threatened to come and get him up every morning if he didn't come to school. Both Dora and Dolan were good kids, but with Donna working nights they had no one to watch them, help them with their homework, or mainly just be there to love them. I didn't blame them or Donna. It was a crappy deal all the way around, but I knew I had to get the kids through their senior year and put a diploma in their hand so they could at least have a chance.

"Donna, how old are you if you don't mind me asking?" I said while she was writing down my order for sweet tea and lemon.

"Mr. Masters I'm thirty-five going on ninety. I imagine right now I look like some raggedy old hag." She flipped her hair back out of her face and spoke in a tone of resignation.

"Your kids are doing well in school you know. You have that to be proud of, " I offered trying to encourage her.

"I am proud of those kids, but I can't send them to college. They'll just wind up like me working for some minimum wage job and I hate that. I hate I can't provide better for them. She was getting fairly emotional and I imagined a lot had to do with her fatigue and the overbearing weight of being a single mom.

Looking around at an otherwise empty dining room I asked, "Why don't you bring me the chicken fry with cream gravy and I want fries on the side. Can you sit down and eat with me at least until someone else wanders in?

"Tommy's gone and the cook is the only one here so I don't see why not. I'd have to get up if we do have any other customers," She said almost relived by the idea of sitting down.

"Okay, the chicken fry for me and you get whatever you want, my treat. Deal?" I asked trying to get a smile out of her.

"Look, I know you aren't trying to get into my britches since when I offered last time you turned me down. So what is it you want?" she asked suspiciously.

"Actually, I thought I might interview you for a job if you want or you can just have dinner and we can call it friends out for lunch. No strings attached I promise." I said holding up my hand as being sworn in on a bible. Something she was more than familiar with.

She half smiled at me and turned to walk back into the kitchen. In a few minutes she came back with my sweet tea and a coffee for her. We sat and sipped our drinks in silence for about five minutes before the bell on the counter rang signaling our order was ready. Donna got up and brought back a large plate of chicken fried steak with cream gravy and French fries on the side. She had ordered herself a club sandwich cut in fourths and poked through with a toothpick. When she had placed the food on the table she sat down and for the longest moment simply closed her eyes. I thought she might be praying, but realized, she rarely had the chance to be a customer anywhere and may have never been a guest period. I think she was savoring the opportunity to just sit and not have one person expecting anything from her. I left her alone as I peppered my gravy and squirted a large pool of catsup alongside the fries on my plate. After I had taken a bite or two, Donna opened her eyes, smiled at me and began to eat.

There was no conversation during the entire meal and thankfully no other customers came in. When we had finished, I sat playing with a toothpick while she cleared the table, and came back with a slice of coconut cream pie for me and a slice of lemon for her.

"My treat!" she said, smiling.

Who's gonna turn down coconut cream pie? I ate my slice in about four bites as she very delicately scraped slice after slice of lemon filling onto her fork and into her mouth. It was if she was trying to make the moment last as long as she possibly could. She got up to refill her coffee and bring me a coffee as well. I put in half and half from a couple of the little plastic cartons and we sipped our coffee as if it was Napoleon brandy.

"Look, Donna," I said as we sat there enjoying the quiet. "I don't know how much you make here, but I have a secretary's position at the school opening up and I would be interested in hiring you. It would be a salary and you would work eight to four, five days a week. You could also be home with your kids at night and on weekends. If you took the job and were at the school, it would give you the opportunity to see your kids participate in school events and have a few good times with them while you still have the chance. You're way too young to be as old as you are right now. "

She looked at me for the longest without saying a word. I wasn't sure if she felt insulted or if she wasn't sure what to do.

34

"You know I don't have any experience or a degree right?" she finally said. "How much would a job like that pay?"

"Donna, this would be considered a paraprofessional position and you wouldn't need a degree. As smart as you are, you would be able to catch on real fast. I imagine the pay would be around $18,000 a year for someone with no experience and you could get insurance for you and your family through the school. How does that stack up against this job?" I asked not really sure what a person might make waiting tables plus tips and of course the nights going out to the sleeper cabs.

"With steady tips and an occasional bonus, I clear $20,000, but the hours are getting to me and in the long run it's not worth the extra few dollars. I still can't send my kids to college though." She had placed her hands under her chin and looked like a schoolgirl as she looked towards the dirty dishes on our table with a thousand yard stare brought on by fatigue and desperation. She just sat there looking and slightly shaking her head. I could guess what thoughts were going through her mind and none of them were happy. As good a person as she was, she needed some happy.

"Donna. Do you trust me?" I asked and it took a little bit of time for her to nod that she did, not that she had to decide, but mainly it was that nothing was registering very quickly right now. "Good. When you finish your shift, tell your boss you're done and get you final check. Go home and sleep until in the morning. Tomorrow morning, get the kids up and ready for school and you come with them when they come. Dress pretty conservative. Be best not to have too much skin or cleavage showing all right? It might intimidate the other ladies." I said with a smile to make it sound less critical. She smiled back knowing I was asking her not to look like a whore. I reached over and took both her hands, "I will have someone there that will train you and we will get you started tomorrow. This will be a good thing for you and your family. My folks will help you get started and you'll be fine. Don't worry about it, okay?"

She finally looked up and had a half smile on her face that had managed to fight though the bone deep fatigue. I suspect that a few happy thoughts of hope and happiness had also begun to overtake the blackness that was her future a few minutes ago. I reached in my billfold and remembered I had emptied it of twenties for the honeymoon couple this morning and hadn't stopped by the bank. I slipped my emergency hundred out from behind my driver's license as I stood up and handed it to Donna for the meals and told her to use the rest to help her get started in her new job. She squeezed my hand as I stood by the table and said thank you. The look on her face was enough. I saw some sparkle back in her eyes. I squeezed her hand back and told her not to be late as I turned and headed out the door.

IX.

Fortunately the bank was between the truck stop and the school so I pulled up next to the ATM to reload my wallet. This charitable giving business was getting expensive, but it was quite gratifying I had to admit. For a day that had started so horribly wrong, I found myself humming along as Jimmy Buffet sang my personal anthem, *Come Monday.* 'Hmm... mm...mmm, I'll be alright, hmmm... mmm...mmm.... just want you back by my side' I managed to hit most of the words as I guided the truck back out on the highway and headed back to Shasta High.

I walked into the office a lot happier man than when I left and the pep in my step was noticeable as Ms. Shelly smiled and said, "So you lived to fight another day it seems and looking at the front of your shirt you had cream gravy with your chicken fry." She followed me into my office and took a Kleenex to my shirt to try and make me presentable. "By the way, we can't go to the lake this weekend, its prom." She stated while she dabbed spit onto the Kleenex.

"Prom? That's this weekend? Hmmmm. I had forgotten." I said, more than a little disappointed as the green bikini slowly faded from my memory. "Wait. How did you forget that? My forgetting is normal, but that's why I have you around."

"I know. I was so disappointed in myself for not having checked the calendar. I guess I just had my mind set on the lake and honestly I think I've been around you too long and some of it's rubbing off, which is kind of scary," she said with a mock shiver.

"I don't know if that's such a bad thing after all," I stated with some mock indignation. "You're always trying to get me to straighten up and grow up a little, to act more mature. Maybe, just maybe you need to lighten up and loosen up some and meet me halfway."

She placed her thumb and index finger on my chin and lifted it slightly like a mom talking to an unruly child, "What scares me is if I start acting more like you, I'll find myself with my legs above my head in some motel room on a school night." Her smile had more devil than fear in it and she playfully slapped my face as she turned and made an exaggerated exit strutting her well-developed stuff.

"Hey wait a minute," I called just as she got to my door. "Do you want to go to prom with me this weekend?"

"You ask a girl this hot (she licked her thumb and placed it on her hip she had jutted out and made a sizzling noise) six days before prom and expect her to still be available?" she asked in perfect southern belle reminiscent of Scarlett herself.

"I'll buy you a flower," I offered sweetening the pot.

"A Gladiola?" She said softening and acting a little more interested.

"Two of 'em!" I stated as if I had made the final winning bid.

"You have to pick me up at my house, come to the door and ring the bell, not honk. You better have on a tie and socks that match, preferably black!" she listed like a diva giving out the requirements needed to breathe her air.

"The tie or the socks?" I asked pretending to take notes.

"The tie or the socks what?" She answered.

"Preferably black. " I said repeating her instructions.

"Both!" she said with a huff and whirled on her heels indignant at having to explain and then swooped out. In about five seconds she peeked back around the door smiling and asked, "Can you pick me up early enough so we can get a plate of enchiladas first?"

"You got it." I said with a big thumbs up.

I had just sat down at my desk when I remembered Donna. I walked back out into the office and said, "By the way I hired Regina's replacement while I was out. She will be here tomorrow to train. I just have to get the paperwork over to HR and let them know. When Regina comes back from lunch you can tell her that she should be able to have her trained in a couple of days and then she can take off. I know she's eager to move back home to take care of her mom.

"Great, do I know her?" She asked

"Donna Clinton. She works out at the truck stop and has two kids here in school." I explained pleased with myself.

Shelly's only reaction was a raised right eyebrow.

"She's the perfect choice. Her kids never made it to school so she can be in charge of getting kids here like hers. She should know what its like. Right? Plus she needed a new job if she's going to have a chance to make anything of herself." I defended my choice vigorously.

"Hmmmm huh" was the only comment Shelly made to this.

"Look she's a good person in a bad situation and no she doesn't have the best reputation, but she is a mother that can make something of herself with your help and her kids will benefit. Will you help her get started?" I asked

"So you hire her and I'm supposed to raise her?" Her eyebrow still arched.

"Do you remember how surprised we were when we looked at Dora's test scores and realized she was brilliant smart? I looked up Donna's scores and she's the same way. It's no fluke. Like mother like daughter. No, she hasn't used good judgment when it came to keeping her legs together, but she' been paying a real high price since then. I just know she'll be great when she gets started and feels at home. She's learned a lot of life lessons the past few years and I bet she has developed a lot of common sense to go along with her natural intelligence. She may even be able to do my job!"

Both eyebrows arched now as she asked, "You want me to go there? Seriously? Yes, she probably knows how to screw around and get herself in trouble well enough to do your job. I agree. Now whether she can do Regina's job, that's another question."

I couldn't help but laugh and then she did too. Shelly agreed to make Donna feel at home and offered to guide her towards respectability. I went back to my office and called Sylvia Benson, the district curriculum director. She had the honor of currently being also in charge of HR, which was a job that was critical in nature, but was passed around like a hot potato to the next new person that was hired. Human resources and curriculum, Super Dan believed, went hand in hand since the people hired did the teaching. He didn't seem to remember the bus drivers, cafeteria workers, maintenance men, or other no instructional people. His argument justified his giving the responsibility to Sylvia along with not giving her a raise 'since it was all part of the same job'.

I explained to Sylvia I had found a new attendance clerk and would be faxing over her application along with my recommendation. I verified that she was someone with 8 years of clerical experience so she would be making $20,301 according to the district salary schedule. She agreed and assured me she would have her started on payroll by tomorrow since I had asked nice and also had done most of the paperwork for her. I didn't have the heart to tell Sylvia I had filled out the application myself and decided that Donna had done a lot of clerical work over the past few years balancing books, balancing her life, and balancing on the console in a few trucks. It was pocket change for the district, but life changing for her. If anyone ever checked, Donna could honestly say she hadn't lied. Hopefully I would be long gone by then.

Just as I was about to call Mary Nell McKenzie, our school counselor, about scholarships for Dora, Shelly buzzed my phone.

"Kelsey and Kneisha are here to see you. Do you have a minute?' She asked.

"Sure, now's good. Would you see if Mary Nell is in her office and have her come see me as well?" I asked.

"The girls are heading your way and I saw Mary Nell going down the hall, but I'll catch her when she comes back through," she said as she hung up.

"Hey Mr. Masters!" Kelsey and Kneisha chimed together as they bounced into my office. They were the definite leaders of the student body. Both were athletes, cheerleaders, and president or vice-president alternately of every major club or organization we had. Their enthusiasm reflected in their voice and their decibel level stayed somewhere between jet plane and rock concert. I at first thought they both had hearing problems until I figured out that they spent all their time addressing groups, cheering at games, or shouting instructions on the court. It just became natural. I dealt with it.

"Hey girls, I haven't seen you since, well let me see, hmmm, oh yeah, first thing this morning! What's going on now?" I kidded them. It was necessary for us to visit two or three times a day, just so they could keep things running smoothly and for me to know what was actually going on. I would almost give them a blank check and tell them to do what they thought was best and save a lot of meetings, but even with Kelsey and Kneisha, I liked my job too much to give that much power away. So we met regularly.

"We have a problem with prom!" Kneisha shouted.

"There's no problem, I'm coming and I found a date just now. All is well!" I said, hoping to lighten up their somber mood.

"Well, good for you," Kelsey said with just a little bit or sarcasm, "Now you need to help us with other people's dates. "

"Okay, what's wrong with other people's dates?" I asked not really wanting to know what was fixing to be shared with me.

"Well it's like this," Kneisha began reporting. "We are charging $25 per person for the tickets or $40 a couple. You know since a guy has a date it won't break him having to buy two tickets, along with a limo or something. It was supposed to be a good thing, but then we started getting everyone buying couples tickets!"

"That is a good thing right? We have more people coming with dates and more fun dancing right?" I asked not seeing the problem.

"NO it's not!" Kelsey jumped in still irritated with the whole mess and me. "Two girls or two boys are signing up as a couple so they can get the tickets cheaper and save money. It's the guys and girls that don't have dates that are pretending they are coming together and Ms. Scoggins, our senior sponsor, is telling them they can't have tickets. It got so bad this morning with the yelling we had to shut down ticket sales and some of the kids say they are going to sue because we are discriminating!"

"Here's what you do, have the guys kiss each other to prove they are actually in love and if they will, surely they deserve a discount don't you think?" I asked with mock seriousness.

"Can we do that?" Asked Kneisha in all seriousness hopeful for a solution.

"Unfortunately, no. Do you girls know what GLAD is?" I asked.

"It's the opposite of sad!" Kelsey once again chimed in with a little edge to her tone.

"Actually that's one answer, but the one I'm looking for is the acronym for the gay and lesbian advocates and defenders. They are very close by and have gone into schools near here that have in some way prevented students from participating because of their sexual preferences. This would be a perfect opportunity for them to visit Shasta if for some reason there is actually one couple in our high school that is truly a same sex couple and we deny them access to the prom. I'm thinking if that happened the mayor, half the school board, and a large number of parents would stroke out if we were required to have a rainbow club in our school or risk losing federal funds."

"So what do we do now?" Kneisha asked frustrated.

"Have you sold any couples tickets yet?" I asked hoping for a negative answer.

"No, the real couples usually wait until the last minute and those hoping to get a date are waiting as well. The only ones that have asked are the boy couples and a few girl-girl couples that heard someone talk about getting cheaper tickets. Word started spreading and they all lined up to buy the couple tickets this morning before school. That's when Ms. Scoggins shut us down," Kneisha reported.

"Here's the solution. You ready? $22. 50. All tickets the same price no matter whether they buy one or six. Anyone wanting to go goes and no questions asked. Tell Ms. Scoggins the same public display of affection rules applies to all couples and she need not worry about having to watch two guys kissing or holding hands or girls for that matter. Okay? We set? Any more issues for today. There's still a few minutes left of this Monday," I asked wishing for a resounding no. Enough was enough and this day needed to end.

41

"Okay, Mr. Masters, we can work with that if Ms. Scoggins can. We will go make new signs and have them up by in the morning when we sell tickets again. Thaaaaaanks!" They said in unison.

"If Ms. Scoggins has an problem with my solution, tell her the only other option would be for her to be the Rainbow Club sponsor," I said indicating I wasn't joking and she needed to buy into this solution.

"Got it!" They said as they bounced out of the office once more on a mission.

X.

It was only after getting Donna lined out and solving another of Kelsey and Kneisha's dilemmas did I remember I was supposed to be calling Abigail Fisher and groveling at her feet. She was probably even madder now since I am sure Thelma called her before lunch to let her know to start gloating and then here I have put her off for several hours. Making her wait would not help matters. Crap. I had better have something good for Super Dan and my plan to work. I picked up the phone and dialed.

"Hello." Abigail's voice over the phone even sounded like her panties were perpetually in a wad.

"Ms. Fisher, this is William Masters up at Shasta High, do you have a minute to talk?" I asked trying to sound humble.

"Mr. Masters, I believe the last time we talked you insulted me in a very nasty way. I'm not sure I would ever choose to talk to you again," she stated wanting to get the most out of what she knew would be me apologizing since Aunt Thelma had put in the fix.

"Yes ma'am, I understand and that's why I am calling. I believe I owe you an apology," I said feeling nauseous as I said the words.

"You feel like you need to apologize or Dan Cochran told you to apologize," she asked laying one of those female traps where there's no right answer.

"Ms. Fisher, Mr. Cochran and I did visit about the whole unfortunate situation and we both came to the conclusion that in the best interest of everyone involved, an apology was called for.

42

I have been giving it some considerable thought the last two hours, making sure I was able to sincerely make you feel that I am repentant," I answered her trick question with a trick answer and hopefully she was too vain to see it.

"Well, I have been expecting a phone call most of the afternoon. It did appear as if you were making me wait and I haven't been happy about that." She scored a couple more points as she continued counting coup on my head. "But if you are willing to apologize, I should at least be willing to listen."

I clenched my teeth and held my tongue while making sure I had control of what I was actually going to say. What was racing through my mind was 'Abigail, I am sorry you are a tight assed bitch that men in this town so despise that you couldn't get laid if you taped balloons to your naked ass, ran a half priced special, and gave out coupons', but then that would pretty much be nuking my career along with Ms. Shelly, my friends, and Super Dan as collateral damage. Instead, I heard myself say in a voice even I thought was fraught with guilt, "I really appreciate that Abigail. May I call you Abigail?" She agreed that since I would be handing her my balls in a silver case we should be on a first name basis from here on out. I continued, "I was way out of line this morning and I let my emotions get the best of me. I should have recognized you were only in here on behalf of your son and that's what its all about, the kids right?" Once again she agreed with enthusiasm working up to what I am sure would be orgasmic glee when she actually heard the words 'I'm sorry'. "I haven't been myself lately, with this year coming to a close, and I took the opportunity to unleash my frustrations on you, which was very unfair. I can say with all sincerity..." I could mentally hear her panting and begin a small, but discernable 'yes, yes, give it to me, yes', "that I am truly sorry for my actions."

There was a pause when I had finished and I am sure she was catching her breath after her mental orgasm having brought another man to his knees. Finally, she said rather softly and almost seductively, "Billy, you know I appreciate that. We don't have to be enemies. As a matter of fact I think we could become very good friends, don't you?"

"Abigail, working together for the good of your son and the other kids would give me great pleasure. Hopefully we can get together real soon. You have a good afternoon, you hear, I have some crazy kid running up and down the hall streaking. I had better go."

"Billy, thank you so much for being the bigger man and calling, you really are … the bigger man and I won't forget it." She ended coyly. "Bye, now. "

I hung up and took a deep breath. I then took a disinfectant tissue and wiped off my phone and my ear. I had a warm Diet Dr. Pepper sitting on my desk from who knows when, but I used it to rinse out my mouth. A man has to do certain things and this was one of them. It was for the greater good I told myself and I would live to fight another day. I just couldn't get the taste of bile out of my mouth.

When the bell finally rang ending the class day and Boomer reported the last bus had left, I walked out to the front office to check on Ms. Shelly.

"Tonight's your book club?" I asked already knowing the answer.

"Yea, I'm excited. We are starting a new book by a former principal. It looks funny and I think I will be able to relate to a lot of the stories." She was talking as she shut down her computer and began clearing her desk to leave for the night.

"Good. You'll have to let me know if it's any good. I might want to read it. I have a few stories of my own and I might just think about writing a book myself," I said, acting as if I might actually read a book, much less write one.

"I'm thinking this book can actually be read by people under twenty-one. I'm not sure your book would be rated PG-13 or the stories you would tell would appeal to anyone other than those that have subscriptions to girlie magazines," she huffed.

"Well now that kind of hurts my feelings. I have an honest appreciation for the feminine population and consider myself a connoisseur. Beside, it's my bad boy image that attracts you isn't it? I believe I heard you say so yourself." I asked knowing I couldn't hold a candle to some of the bad boys Ms. Shelly had tried to salvage.

"Lets just say I keep hanging out with you because you have ... potential!" she smiled as she came up with the descriptor she thought fit.

"Let's just say I hang out with you because you have a nice ass!" I responded back.

"I rest my case from the earlier argument," was all she said.

"That and the fact I am madly in love with you," I added.

"Potential means that maybe next time you will lead with that one and we will live happily ever after. Right now I'm off to change before the meeting. I'm hosting tonight and have to get my snacks set out," She gave my hand a quick squeeze as Mary Nell came through the door. "See you tomorrow okay?"

"I'll be at home watching the Rangers game behaving myself. See you tomorrow," I promised as I gave her a wink as she left and I turned to Mary Nell.

"Mary Nell. Just the person I wanted to see," I said.

"I heard you were looking for me. What's up? Cheerleaders?" Said asked hoping for a 'no'.

"Thank God, no. The Cheerleaders are all fine as far as I know and if they aren't, don't tell me. What I need is scholarships. Can we look and see what, if anything, we can get Dora Simmons, Donna Clinton's daughter, in the way of financial aid or something. We need that kid in college. Donna is going to start working up here tomorrow and I promised we would do everything we could to help her get her kids into college," I asked with a small measure of hope.

"Well, the thing about scholarships is you have to start early and financial aid grants have deadlines. Starting this late, there wouldn't be much chance for this year, but..." I started to have a sinking feeling wondering what other options I had, "that's why Dora and I started way back in the fall. We've already been working on the paper work and it was going to be her surprise for her mom. Not only does she qualify for financial aide, but also her scores have earned her some big bucks for academic scholarships. We will announce all that at graduation. Anything else I can help you with?" she asked with a broad smile on her face, very pleased with herself.

"Well Mary Nell, you just earned yourself a big hug and I imagine a bigger budget for next year. Thank you. I really appreciate that and I know her momma will be so proud," I said sincerely grateful for having good people around me.

I checked my watch and decided enough was enough as I locked my door and left the building. I drove through the window at The Rib Shack and got a slab of slow cooked pork ribs with a side of coleslaw and beans. Along with more than one cold beer, this would be my supper in front of the television. The Rangers were starting a home stand against the Angels tonight and had a new young pitcher throwing. I expected to see a good ball game and fall asleep in my chair. This Monday was a goner. I tallied the goods and the bads in my head and decided we won today. That was what it was all about. Staying one step ahead of losing. I snuck one rib out of the bag to chew on as I drove home listening to Merle Haggard sing *That's the Way Love Goes.* Things could be worse.

Prom

I.

I wouldn't admit this to anyone, but I really liked prom and I say that having worked almost twenty of them. They are never boring, but it's always a fun evening. The kids dress up and their actions, though many times still juvenile, take on a more classy approach as if the tuxes and fancy dresses raise their level of consciousness and their actions become more inspired, but in a good way.

I had pulled into Ms. Shelly's drive at 5:55, parked, and strolled up to the door with a corsage box in my hand. I hadn't gone black tie since I barely own a suit and a couple of sports coats, but I did wear my favorite blue tie and made sure my socks were black. At least I thought they were. I had a hard time with the fine line between navy blue and black so on more than one occasion I had shown up in black slacks with blue socks to school. When Shelly answered the door and gave me the once over, I pulled up the legs of my slacks so she could see in the sunlight and got a thumbs up on the socks.

Having passed inspection, I took a look at Shelly and as always, she took my breath away. She never ceased to amaze me with what she wore. At work she maintained a basic functional office wardrobe and then when we were out for fun, she loved her jeans. And when baby had her blue jeans on, well that was some serious fun. On occasion, she and I had snuck over to Dallas or Oklahoma City where we were less conspicuous as a couple and had a fancy dinner or two. Each time when she walked out, I was stunned at the change in her appearance and demeanor with an evening gown on. Tonight was a favorite of mine since it was her classic black dress. She had on her diamonds that graced her ears and around her neck. The one obvious place on her finger remained bare. I did need to fix that.

As she walked across the room and turned like a model on a catwalk, I resisted the immature approach of whistling and clapping, but chose instead to bow in her direction. I offered to pin on her corsage, but she felt it best that she do it right the first time. She knew that even all dressed up; when I slid my hand under the strap of her dress to keep from poking her I might forget what I was doing. She sometimes didn't give me much credit, but then my credit score wasn't that high to begin with.

We made a quick trip to Decatur to get a plate of enchiladas before I needed to be in place to start my evening of monitoring. Decatur had one of the best Mexican food restaurants around, but the fine citizens of Shasta refused to go there so Shelly and I were safe. It was like having two Baptist running into each other at a bar. Both knew they were safe since the other person couldn't burn them without burning himself. If anyone had ever seen us in Decatur they couldn't share it since it would incriminate them in the process. So we ate and enjoyed each other's company in a non-business setting. These were the times we actually could talk about things we liked and dreams we had. It never got old and I enjoyed her company immensely. After three beef enchiladas, beans and rice, Shelly felt like she was ready for an evening of standing on her feet until almost 1 A. M so I paid and we drove back toward Shasta.

II.

I'm not sure who started the tradition, it could actually go all the way back to the 1800's for all I know, but most schools hold their prom at hotels. I find that ironic and amusing. The justification was a hotel was usually one of the few places with a large enough meeting hall that could also double as a dance floor. Most folks chose to focus on those attributes. As a principal, I am constantly amazed at how much parents chose to ignore in the name of the almighty prom. The first of course is the dress they let little Susie pick out that showed most of her breasts, half her butt, and if she's not careful, revels her deepest darkest secret. After that we get to the dancing, which parents watch as sponsors and see their children basically having sex standing up in their clothes. Hopefully in their clothes. By the end of the night when it's really dark, I am never sure.

But getting their kids a room takes the prize. Lets get Bobby or Nancy a room so they can go and change after supper or before the dance. Lets get them a room so they don't have to drive home after the dance and risk falling asleep. Duh. You buy a high school kid a room at a hotel the night they are all dressed up and spend hours rubbing their bodies up against their date with their private areas of excitement separated by only a fractions of an inch of silk or nylon. Then put a room key in their back pocket.... can anyone say 'come up for a drink'? Can anyone say 'unprotected sex'? Can anyone say, 'yes sweetie, you came along exactly nine months to the day of my high school prom. You were the parting gift. When I parted, I got the gift.' Heaven help us. I have raised thousands of kids over the years, none that were my own so maybe I don't understand why parents go totally stupid when they need to be the smartest.

Regardless, I pulled into the parking lot at the Claymore Hotel on Ross Street. It was Shasta's oldest hotel and had some wear and tear to it, but it still tried to maintain a dignified manner. Every living generation of Shasta graduates still remembered having their prom at the Claymore. It was three stories tall and the main ballroom was a throwback to the roaring twenties with large chandeliers glistening overhead. Huge tapestries hung on the walls and when the lights were dimmed, a person could almost imagine a scene out of *The Great Gatsby.* The set up made for a nice area where students could sit and visit next to the large ballroom floor, which was a holdover from generations long gone, but made the Claymore the ideal place for a ball or prom. The very features that dated it, were the ones that came back to serve the public best at these times. My personal favorite was the long circle driveway that led to the front door. Tonight it had been cordoned off and decorated to resemble the red carpet during the Oscars, including having bleachers set up for the paparazzi.

Of course the paparazzi tonight were the parents, the reporter from the Shasta Daily News, now printed twice a week, and quite a few towns people that considered this one of the highlights of Shasta society for the year. The arrival of the students was greeted with oohs and ahhs for the mode of transportation they chose, followed by an emcee that announced the individual or couple. Photos were snapped in rapid succession accompanied by comments on dresses or hairstyles as the students strolled through the flashing lights feeling like

Hollywood's elite. Sometimes one of the guys would wear a Tux or suit that was out of the ordinary and make the crowd mummer, but mainly the compliments and catty remarks were reserved for the girls and the prom dress or lack of it that they had picked out. The pressure on moms and girls was immense this time of year and fortunes were spent by many that didn't have fortunes to spend.

The first arrivals were always the younger students or those without a date. They were excited and wanted to get the evening going, but the veterans, especially the girls that had been invited as freshman and were now seniors, knew to the minute when the best window of opportunity was to arrive and sweep in with the most amount of attention and overshadow any others that may try to compete. It definitely was an art and a science, I guess, when you factor in timing, hormones, and genetics.

The parents and a few teachers sponsored the prom with oversight by Ms. Scoggins, the senior sponsor. Boomer was here to handle any discipline problem that might arise, even though we have had only one real problem in twelve years. As back up, we always have a couple of off duty police officers since this is an off campus event and it makes the Claymore feel better about our using their facility. Ms. Shelly and I are mainly here to look pretty and be a presence, which is what makes the night so nice. The crowd is mostly junior and seniors with a few underclassmen sprinkled in that were lucky enough to get asked by an older student so the focus remains on having a good time and very little is thought about acting up or misbehaving.

Ms. Shelly and I parked around the back and walked through the ballroom to get to the main entrance. Our appearance seemed like nothing more than school officials coming out to get the party started as we took our spot next to the door and at the end of the catwalk so as not to block any mother from getting the picture she needed.

We watched as various vehicles pulled up to the drive to expel their occupants and have the valet dads take their car and park it, hanging onto the keys until the students chose to leave for good. Some were the students' cars they regularly drove to school, while some of the younger students were driving borrowed cars belonging to their parents. Early on you would see a station wagon or mini van coming and would know these were the young kids, singles, or groups of friends all coming together for safety in numbers.

As the time slipped well past the appointed beginning of prom, the interesting vehicles made their appearance each trying to out do the next. First, there were town cars and then stretch limos. Several couples had rented a stretch Hummer limo that ran the length of the block and when they unloaded it appeared students piled out for a good five minutes. Covering the cost must have required quite a few participants. One of the cowboys came driving up in a horse drawn buggy and created a dilemma among the dads as far as securing the buggy and ensuring the students didn't leave without checking out first. Our off duty police officer solved the problem by taking a tire boot out of his patrol car and locked up one of the wagon wheels.

The prize for the most unique ride this year went to the couple that arrived in a monster truck with wheels so high a ladder had to be let down for the couple to descend. With the girl's dress being one of the shorter styles, all of us present were able to see the moon come up as she came down. I was thankful she wore panties, as brief as they may have been, as opposed to a thong or au naturèl. We were at least allowed to retain a little of the mystery concerning her posterior. Safely on the ground and reveling in the attention, Moonchild waved and blew kisses as if she were the Rose Bowl Queen, while her date beamed with pride. I'm guessing he was thinking as much about his truck as the girl next to him, but that was just guessing. The dads drew straws for the right to park the monster and off it lurched down the street and around the corner. Hopefully, the lucky dad would have it back by the time the kid needed to leave and not crush any other vehicles or pedestrians along the way.

As the students exited their vehicles, the emcee announced them by name and class, sometimes offering personal comments about the dresses or cars if he knew them well enough. The emcee saw himself as Shasta's own Bert Parks and since this was his thirty-eighth prom, he probably knew their grandparents as well as their parents. As far as we could tell the groups or pairs of same sex students walking the runway were there as friends and none of the "couples" that Kelsey and Kneisha had been so worried about showed or at least as they came up the red carpet it wasn't obvious they were a couple or that they were ready to announce to the town of Shasta their undying love. Considering the conservative nature of the town, staying in the closet until one had the opportunity to move to a more liberal setting was probably advisable. It was even sad that Joe Bob Gordon and Chastity Wheeler came separate with friends and would spend the entire evening never once speaking or dancing even though they were married. It amazed me the narrow mindedness that existed in some places that prided themselves on being shut off from the world and considered living in the past a virtue.

Shelly enjoyed seeing the girls and every one stopped and hugged her or spoke. She was their mother at school and looked after ever girl as if they were her daughter. She beamed with pride seeing the beautiful dresses and hair and I tried not to spend too much time worrying about the cleavage and the slits up the sides of the dresses. I spoke to the guys occasionally and complimented them for cleaning up nice and encouraged them to treat their date like the lady she appeared to be tonight. For some I really should have said treat her better than how she appears tonight. She may look like a slut, but she is someone's daughter. As they left later in the evening, Shelly and I would retake our position by the door and remind them to go straight home, not drink and drive, and behave. The majority smiled and lied right to our face.

III.

When the stars for the night finally arrived and more students were inside than out, we moved into the darkness and I sought out the punch bowl. My purpose was twofold; quench our thirst and to make sure an adult or two was present and the punch was served to the students a glass at a time. No one dipped out of the bowl but sponsors. I had learned this lesson the hard way. In the past, I had a student or two spike the punch with Vodka or Everclear, but by the time we knew about it, the bowl was empty and the party was rocking. No harm no foul. We learned that when a large group of students hit the punch bowl all at once, word had spread that the good stuff was on the table. I never worried too much about that even though I probably should have. The dilution rate was so low that no one kid was going to get enough to even have much more than a placebo effect, which usually happened with freshmen. Someone tells them the punch is spiked and the next thing you know they are having trouble walking or talking until Boomer shows up and starts quizzing them. He has sobered up many students and a few adults.

We started monitoring the punch bowl my second year at Shasta when Tommy 'I'm a rebel without a cause and too stinking lazy to come up with my own so I'm just going to cause people grief and call it anarchy' Lucas moved in. He, of course, came to prom in jeans and a t-shirt proclaiming the party was the work of an elite fascist society and he wouldn't conform. He just came by to have some of the strawberries dipped in chocolate and a few cookies while making it known what mindless cattle everyone else was for following such materialistic traditions. None of that fazed anyone and most ignored Tommy as they went about the business of being elitist and materialistic. Boomer stayed close to him at first, but after a while he seemed harmless.

About halfway through the prom we noticed an odd effect ripple through the crowd. No one was anywhere near the punch bowl and many were chunking their glasses of punch into the trash. This registered, in my highly trained mind, as a potential problem. I looked to where I had seen Boomer last and caught a glimpse of him dragging Tommy through one of the side doors into a hall. I started that way wondering what on Earth had happened. When I made my way across the dance floor and pushed on the door it wouldn't open. I heard scuffling coming from behind the door even with the music blaring so I shouted to see if Boomer was okay. The scuffling stopped and a few seconds later the door opened wide enough for me to slip through. When I made it into the hall and looked around the door, it was evident what had caused the obstruction- Tommy Lucas. Boomer had him by the shoulders of his t-shirt dangling him about four feet off the ground and pressed against the door. He basically was strangling him with the crew neck of the shirt that had ridden up under Tommy's chin as his face turned redder and redder. His feet were dangling and kicking, seeking solid ground on which to stand and give him some much needed oxygen.

"Boom, I'm thinking maybe we need to let Tommy down, what do you think?" I asked as if this was a democratic meeting.

Boomer was eyeball to eyeball with Tommy and as red as Tommy's face was, Boomer's was redder. I didn't see a lot of good coming from this and probably needed to bring it to a close pretty soon.

"Boom. Boomer, buddy. Hey big guy. Let's ease up a little and step back. I need you to report on what's going on." I encouraged as I patted his arm a little firmer with each stroke. Finally, Tommy's body began sliding down the door until his feet reached the ground. Boomer gave him enough room to stand and breathe, but moved so close to him, if Tommy thought of bolting or even moving, Boomer was prepared to squash him like a bug.

"I drank his pee!" the words came out of Boomer's mouth like the guttural sound made by an angry grizzly.

I looked at Boomer and then at Tommy who was doing nothing, but taking shallow breaths and looking at Boomer, hoping Boomer would have a heart attack, before he finished Tommy off.

"You drank his pee?" I asked trying to sound casual and inquisitive.

Nothing. Boomers breathing was still labored and face still red. His eyes bored into Tommy and if looks could have killed...

"He spiked the punch bowl with pee!" Boomer finally was able to offer further explanation. "And I DRANK some! I've dealt with this little shit all year and let him live long enough to come to prom, but I'm thinking you don't want to be here for the rest of this. I can handle it from here." Boomer offered in a very strange and cold sounding way.

"Tommy, buddy, you spike the punch bowl?" I asked hoping to get a dialogue going.

"I told my friends I did as a joke, but I didn't put anything into the punch. I just pretended to. The cup I came out of the bathroom with was just lemonade. I swear!" Tommy was explaining and pleading for his life.

"BULLSHIT!" was all that came out of Boomer's mouth shouted right into Tommy's face. A face that was starting to look younger and more scared as the minutes past. I'm thinking his anarchy days were numbered one way or other.

"It's true. I didn't put anything into the punch! I swear!" And then he saved his own life by beginning to cry. Even Boomer eased up a little when it dawned on him he was holding a scrawny sixteen year old in his huge hands with menace on his mind. The tears kind of refocused the whole situation.

"Tell you what Boom. You go find me one of those police officers and I will stay here with Tommy. We probably will give him a ride home. Okay?" I asked softly and nudged him as I spoke.

"That's probably a good idea. I'll be right back. Will you be alright?" he asked as he handed Tommy over to me.

"I think we'll be fine until you get back," I assured him as he slipped through the door and into the ballroom.

I motioned for Tommy to sit on the floor, which he did without hesitation. "Tommy, we are going to work this out, but I need to know if maybe you have had enough rebelling? This time just about ended your young life before you've had a chance to really start living."

"I didn't do anything wrong," he said feebly, the defiance in him having a hard time letting go.

"Tommy, I can turn you back over to Boomer when he gets back or I can send you home. You messed up big time tonight and the first step to actually growing up is admitting making a mistake. Which do you want to do?"

Time passed for what seemed like an eternity. Finally Tommy spoke, "Okay, maybe I messed up everybody's party. They all hate me anyway."

"Tommy. People wouldn't hate you if you didn't try so hard to make them. Give people a chance and you might find that you have some friends. Quit being such a jerk all the time."
I counseled, whether it would do any good or not, I had no idea. "Here's the deal. You will go home with the police officer and

56

stay home until school is out next week. If you want to come back in the fall, it had better be with a new attitude. As far as Mr. Boomer and you, I'd forget that part and just be thankful you are still alive and breathing. I wouldn't want him to come looking for you. Tell your dad what ever you want, but let it be known you messed up and got suspended. If he calls me up, I may have to tell him the truth so make it good. Can you do that?" I asked hoping he was willing to let bygones be bygones and start his summer vacation a week early.

"So I don't have to go to school no more this year? I just stay home and that's it?" He asked as if I had just told him he had won the lottery and was going on tour with Limp Bizkit.

"Only if you agree to forget how angry you made Mr. Boomer. Got it?" I demanded.

"Yes, sir. " He said actually being polite for the first time I had known him.

The police officer came and called a squad car to give Tommy a ride home. I never heard a word about the incident in the hall and when the next year started, we received a records request from Arkansas where Tommy had gone to live with his Mom. I hope he stayed out of prison and the cemetery. I sometimes wondered. Bottom line? Nobody gets near the punch bowl, but adult sponsors. We call that the Tommy Lucas rule.

IV.

With our cups of punch in our hands, Ms. Shelly and I began a routine that would last for the next three hours. We would walk a few steps along the walls, pause for a few minutes and then move again. We did this to be visible to the kids and also to never stand in one place long enough for a parent to come up and ask a question or tell me about a problem. Sip and stroll. Sip and stroll. Let the good times roll.

Ms. Scoggins did a good job of picking parents to be sponsors and stuck with her criteria faithfully. They had to be on the lenient side and have a sense of humor. She learned this the hard way one year when a fully devoted Presbyterian mom came to sponsor and about an hour into the dancing, fainted dead away right after she was heard mumbling about Satan's hordes. At least they thought she said hordes. We monitored and would have stopped any behavior that violated my two rules, which is no unauthorized body parts may be visible and no unauthorized handling of unauthorized body parts. Other than that, knock yourself out. And they did.

My first few years, the circle gave me alarm. The kids gathered around dancers that did solos and showed off their moves as a couple. It became a ring of bodies and pretty much blocked from view any activity that could have included nude wrestling and no one other than the students would have known. When I came to Shasta and hired Boomer, I never worried about it again. When you have an assistant that is 6'7" and can part a wall of students like Moses parted the Red Sea, problem solved. The students know that when they circle up, Boomer will be standing right behind them and can see EVERYTHING they do. And of course all they really want to do is dance. I have found that given the chance, students just want to have fun.

Our DJs all come from the Dallas-Fort Worth area where they play dances for a much more diverse group of students. Here in Shasta we have about 85% rednecks, 14. 5% brown necks, and .5% black necks, but that doesn't change their playlist and a heavy dose of Rap is played much to the delight of our three African-American couples that take the lead and help the more country kids loosen up and follow the steps when a mass dance is called for. It's ironic to me that I spent hours trying to coordinate student movements for programs or graduation and have some success, but start up the Tootsie Roll song by 69 and every kid at the dance is on the floor, spread out in line, and moving in unison to the instructions in the song. *To the left to the left to the right to the right.*

As country as our kids were, they still had a good selection of Rap CDs stuffed alongside their Taylor Swift and Brad Paisley in their car consoles and on their iPods. I have to admit, having heard so many of the songs at dances and during programs or pep rallies, I had a few that stuck in my head. Whenever Sir Mix A lot starts in with *'I like big butts'* it always earned me a narrow eyed glare and a punch on the arm from Ms. Shelly. I had developed a habit of humming or singing as I moved about the office at school, which I tended to do more when I was in a good mood. Without realizing it, after a dance a few years ago, I had 'big butts' stuck in my head and when I was focused on something else, I found myself singing it several times until one afternoon Ms. Shelly followed me into my office and said, "Seriously? Seriously?"

Caught off guard I asked confused, "What? What happened? What did I do now?"

"Seriously, you don't know?" she asked and I shook my head clueless so she went on. "You've walked around this office for two days singing about how you like big butts and I'm sitting there the whole time in front of people who I'm sure suspect we go out together and how do you think that makes me feel? That you like me because I have a big butt? That you think my butt is big?" She finished pretty fired up and demanding.

I stood there stunned a few seconds but seemed like minutes trying to comprehend what was happening. One minute I'm whistling Dixie minding my own business and the next I have a very irate secretary/lover mad at me. That had to be a first. No, its probably happened before, but it had been a while and never with Ms. Shelly.

"So you are upset because I'm singing a Rap song about big butts?" I asked like a kid answering a question on an oral test hoping he might get close enough for partial credit.

"I'm upset because you are strolling through the office bragging about your taste in big butts and then spend your time with me, ergo, you think I have a big butt," she huffed.

"This is one of those trick questions right? I mean is there actually a right answer? Because I think your butt is great. I've told you that a thousand times, haven't I? And I squeeze it as often as you will let me. I love your butt," I offered hoping any of that might help.

"Billy, for gosh sake, focus. Find a new damn song to sing around the office if you ever want to squeeze my butt again. I am a strong woman, but my butt is proportional to my size and fits me perfectly. I don't want anyone, including you, to refer to it as big. If big butts is what you are really interested in, there are more than a few ladies in this town that can fix you right up!" she turned and stomped back to her desk while I took the opportunity to look at her butt to see if maybe something had changed, but just as I did she yelled without looking back, "You had better not be looking at my butt, mister!" So I stopped, well actually I didn't. I wanted to, but I couldn't help myself.

I finally gave the bizarre behavior enough thought to piece together why she was upset and vowed to myself never to sing or hum that song again and have kept that promise to this day. I can't help, but smile though every time it's played at a dance, which earns me a punch in the arm and a raised eyebrow warning not to say a word. I was so thankful when Dierks Bentley came out with *Am I the Only One* where he mentions '*the country cutie with the rock and roll bootie'.* I memorized the whole verse and sang it a cappella in a very loud voice from my office one morning until Ms. Shelly came smiling to the door. "I love your rock and roll bootie," I said and all was forgiven.

5.

The DJ moved through the usual fare, mixing Rap, country and a few Mexican songs in for our Hispanic kids, and everyone begin to loosen up. The pomp and circumstance of the beginning pageantry was a thing of the past. Dancing and laughing, with a little drama by some of the younger girls, dominated the evening as we moved closer to midnight. I don't know what the Mexican dance was, but when the accordion sound started, everyone began a circle going counter clockwise around the floor. People dance as couples or groups as they slide and twirl. I took Ms. Shelly onto the floor for a couple of these since it was like 'everyone skate' at the roller rink. No one sat out since partners weren't necessary. Just slide along and twirl. Whatever it was, it was fun for everyone. Ms. Shelly was a great country dancer so we couldn't pass up the Cotton Eyed Joe or Schottische and usually went for one two-step and waltz. The kids loved having us on the floor and occasionally one or two of the guys wanted to dance with Ms. Shelly, but we have our own unwritten rules about dances with students. You never knew when they might want to move in close or cop a feel in the name of dancing. The guys would probably do the same to Ms. Shelly.

Ms. Shelly and I had made a couple of circuits around the hotel ballroom and each time we passed the snack tray I picked up another couple of cookies. Ms. Shelly focused on the chocolate fountain and the strawberries. All of this was our fuel for the evening so it was quite necessary to keep us going. We went out into the foyer to watch the photographer snap pictures of couples, groups, individuals, or any assortment the students asked for as a change of pace. As we slowly moved back towards the darken dance floor, Ms. Shelly took the opportunity to powder her nose. I went back inside the ballroom and stood by the door listening to the music that had been ramped up for the last hour with pulsating European techno songs and more of the popular Rap songs.

By now the prim and proper dresses so proudly displayed just a couple of hours earlier were hiked up as the girls ran back and forth between tables or out to the floor for the next dance. Shoes had long been discarded under the tables and bare feet were everywhere. Guys' jackets and cummerbunds were flung over the back of chairs and shirttails were hanging out with few exceptions. Ties were on tables or looped around their heads like sweat bands. The hundred dollar hairdos had long wilted under the heat and sweat of the evening while thousands of bobby pins were strewn across tables with only enough left to keep the hair out of the girls' eyes. We were approaching orgy stage.

Growing up watching Tarzan on television most Saturday mornings, I was often reminded of the scene where the rival tribe inevitably captured the caravan and prisoners were being sacrificed. As the drums beat louder, the intensity heated up driving the villagers into a frenzy just before the native porters, who were always first, were sent flinging by bent over trees. This human carnage continued until the music built as high as it could go and then...Tarzan gave his yell that stifled everything. If only I could yell like Tarzan.

I was thinking about this once again as Flo Rida's *Low Low* played at peak volume and every kid in the room raced to move en mass as they took the floor, then got low, low, low. I actually liked the song and would find myself humming it as well the next few days. It had a way of climbing into your head. I did not know what the words were, but I could under stand the low, low,

low part as I watch the kids perform as if they were a dance team in competition. Funny, Ms. Shelly had never asked to go out and dance this number. Maybe next time. I was smiling to myself thinking about us in the middle of that fanatical mass trying to keep up with the steps and wondering whether I could even get low enough to count when three girls came running up to me with their dresses hiked up. It was Berkley Woods with her entourage of Bay Leigh and Brittney.

"Hey girls. Fun evening?" I greeted them.

"Hey, Mr. Masters," Berkley shouted over the music. "Yea, we're having a great time, but my dress broke and my boob fell out." She reported this in a matter of fact way as if telling me about her cat.

"What?" I asked, since I really couldn't hear being partially deaf and the music being overly loud. Unfortunately, this was mistaken as not comprehending.

"My dress broke and my boob fell out!" Berkley repeated a little louder this time and she demonstrated exactly what happened to help clear up any confusion. She had been holding onto the strap that had supported the right side of her dress and her right boob as well. She let it go, as it must have done when it broke on the dance floor just minutes before and sure enough her boob fell out.

Similar things like this had happened over the course of my career. When I was coaching girls and had to go into the dressing room during half time or before practice to go over game plans or workouts, someone always went over to the bathroom stalls to pee or came out of the stalls as I came through the door. I had been standing in back hallways on more than one occasion talking to a volleyball or basketball coach when the girls would drop their bags and start changing right in front of me including visiting teams.

I asked Coach Connelly about it one time and she said it was nothing, they just didn't recognize me as being part of their world. I asked what that meant and she tried to explain how young girls' minds worked, used imagery as if I were like landscape, and I became too confused to keep up. What I had finally decided was they considered me of no interest, saw me as

62

a non entity, and at no time was any of their actions even close to be considered a come on or flirtation. Had something like that even been mentioned to them, I am sure they would have hooted with laughter, which of course would have hurt my feelings immensely. It seemed best, simply to act unperturbed by it all and be as casual as they were. One piece they didn't factor in was that I was neither dead or blind and when we started talking about some of these high school girls, well fortunately my thoughts couldn't be used in a court of law and I had enough morals to keep them at thoughts.

There was a reason Berkley's strap had broken and their was a reason the term 'fell' was used to described what happed. Berkley was one of the girls that had matured early and quickly. She was beautiful, but as close to a tomboy as I had seen and except for a couple of occasion such as prom, she wore wranglers and boots. She drove her Ford pickup like a bat out of hell and could cuss the boys under a table and I would guess she could drink them there as well. Berkley was also not someone you messed with since she had cleaned the clock of one of the athletes in junior high that had dared pinch her developing boob and asked if it was plastic. The butt whipping lasted until two teachers pulled her off him as she continued to flail away. He couldn't live down the humiliation of being whipped by a girl and the family moved away before the school year ended. The coaches were unhappy since he was projected to be an outstanding football player and was large for his size. He would have done fine as long as he didn't have to line up across from Berkley. Since then no one messed with her and she chose who took her out and what girls hung around with her.

Standing in the dark helped as I looked right into the face of Berkley as she stood there, boob hanging out, and wanting to know if she could go home and fix it quick and come back. Our policy of course was once you leave you don't come back, which was implemented to stop students from going out to the car for a pull on a bottle or a quick smoke. I motioned for her to pull her strap back up and cover up the boob that had been staring at me defiantly. She adjusted as I told her Ms. Shelly would be back in a minute and could help her fasten it well enough to get her

63

through the rest of the dance. Now I had no idea if Ms. Shelly could help her or not, but I did know that I was passing Berkley off as soon as Shelly's nose was powered and she came back in. Regardless of what girls thought about me being landscape, I wasn't dead or immune. The last thing I needed was to be looking at a naked boob belonging to a student. Actually, the last thing I needed was having someone see me looking at a boob belonging to a student. Dark had its advantages.

Fortunately, Ms. Shelly appeared and I quickly explained the situation so Berkley wouldn't have to demonstrate again. Ms. Shelly looked with a raised eyebrow to see if I had been professional or had I enjoyed the show? I raised my hands proclaiming innocence as she led the girls out the door. With the help of a heavy-duty box stapler found by the night clerk at the hotel desk, Berkley was back in action in time for the last few dances of the night. As far as I knew, her boob stayed put and if anyone had witnessed the wardrobe malfunction on the floor except her entourage, they kept their mouth shut. A boob was a boob, but even Berkley's above average boob wasn't worth having to move for.

I remembered going to dances when I was growing up. Rarely did the school sponsor a dance, but usually one was held down at the local community center after football games or the Catholic Church was good for a couple each semester. Catholics could still go to heaven even if they danced and it proved to be a good fundraiser. The best part of the dance that I remembered was towards the end of the evening, the music played by the live local bands or whoever was spinning records, were slow dances. By this time, only couples were left dancing and it gave kids a chance to pull in close to their date and feel their body, which was about as close to each other's body as they would probably be getting that night, but the point was to provide for a romantic finish to the night.

These days? No way! Like I had said, the music built to a frenzied pace and when Ms. Scoggins notified the DJ it was quitting time, the last song usually left the kids panting and sweating in a cluster. And then the lights were brought up, providing much needed visibility, but temporarily blinding everyone until eyes could adjust after three hours or so of almost total darkness. The exit consisted of scrounging around for pieces of clothing that had been discarded over the course of the night and finding shoes.

When the last student had left, a sweep of the room would be made and boxes filled with articles of clothing left behind that could be reclaimed at school on Monday. Guys that had rented tuxes would need all the parts to return them and of course the girls usually came by for belts or whatever may have been forgotten. I am always amazed at how many times we find one shoe. How can someone walk out and forget one shoe. Some of the girls bring their tennis shoes or boots to slip on to go home and I can see leaving a pair of shoes behind, but it never fails that one shoe is under a table and somewhere out there is a girl hobbling long with one shoe on and one off thinking 'something doesn't feel right'.

After we had wished the kids a good night, soliciting promises to behave, knowing some were lying through their teeth, and picked up the room, Ms. Shelly and I strolled out the back way to my truck. It was one of my favorite times of the year, because it's late, dark, warm, and after hours of pulsating music it is so quiet, the crickets can be heard. On more than one occasion, I had walked Ms. Shelly home as opposed to ruining the night by getting inside the truck. We sometimes got lucky and had a large moon to light the way. Tonight the standing had taken a toll on both our feet so we opted to ride. I didn't turn on the CD player and we left the windows down listening to the night and letting the breeze blow through the cab. I heard Ms. Shelly humming to herself as she sat lost in thought. I smiled to myself as I recognized one of the last songs played. Beyonce's *Single Ladies.* I listened and wondered if she was sending me a message or just enjoying the catchy tune. *If you liked it then you should have put a ring on it, If you liked....* I had to think that Ms. Shelly wasn't a very random person. There was something about that song that struck a chord with her and tonight it might be subconscious, but there had to be a time when she gave the lyrics some serious thoughts to be able to sing them word for word. Hmmmmm. Made me wonder, but then maybe I was supposed to.

When I reached her house located in one of the neighborhoods that had homes over a hundred years old, we sat in her porch swing for a few minutes to savor the sounds of the night before I kissed her goodnight and headed out of town.

If I like it then I had better put a ring on it, I like it so I ought put a ring on it.

Last Monday

I.

The last Monday of a school year was a benchmark we all
looked forward to. With semester test occupying most of the last
three days and many of the students being exempt, we really
only had two full days of classes before we started winding up
another year. Most people showed up on this Monday happier
than at any other time during the year.

Graduation was scheduled for Saturday morning and the most
euphoric twenty-four hours of my life would begin immediately
afterwards. Yes! I was mentally going over the ceremony and
the still unfinished plans as I stood in the cafeteria watching the
same kids, come in the same doors, wearing the same shorts and
sandals, at the same time, as they had almost everyday of the
year. As unique as everyone thought they were, most of us were
creatures of habit. The driven students arrived early with all
their gear packed in a bag or backpack bustling through the door
needing to make stops at three different rooms before heading
to practice for.... In two minutes they would be back wanting to
know why Mrs. So and So's room was locked and could I let them
in to drop off a paper, a poster, a plate of brownies for the party
third period, or a whole host of other possibilities. I always did
because the teachers paced themselves and were within days of
surviving another year so most were still a good twenty to thirty
minutes away from gracing the doors of the school.

The students that were the forgetful, artistic, lazy, live by
themselves with no parents on the scene, rolled in every
morning just as the first bell rang to send students to their first
class. They were tucking in shirts, putting on belts, eating a
donut, or wiping the sleep out of their eyes as they made their
way to class. Many stepped through the classroom door just as
the tardy bell rang with a pencil or pen and a piece of paper for
notes. So even their rebellious, non-conformist ways were
traditional and predictable which negated their whole
individually thing and made them actually the masses. I would
never tell them that though because it might crush their spirit.
It's easier to draw the lines wide and let them operate within
wide boundaries as opposed to squeeze everyone into a narrow
chute. All that does it cause everyone grief and no one wins. My

way, the work got done, students graduated, most smiled during the day, and few of us went home with ulcers.

As I continued to analyze the kids that were walking by, I realized they thought the same about me. I stood at the same place in the hall each morning, which gave me a view of the cafeteria, the bus lane, and the main corridor. I drank my same large cup of coffee, which was always ready and waiting for me in the Coffee Café when I rolled in around seven and finished the morning off with peppermint candy. If terrorist put Shasta High on a list of high priority targets, it wouldn't take their top spy to get the lay of the land or figure out schedules. Fortunately, any terrorist that wandered by would be easily identifiable and based on the number of deer rifles and .22s that were in the pick-ups out in the parking lot, we would have a very good chance of holding our own.

With only five days left until graduation and nothing of value in the school other than Mrs. Jefferies coconut crème pie I had seen go by heading for a party in Spanish class, I didn't worry too much about being a target. I did worry that there wouldn't be any pie left by the time I could do an unscheduled walkthrough of Mr. Lopez's classroom and be willing to make time to sample the pie and any other fare that looked good. I tried to never eat food kids brought to school as a rule since I didn't trust even the best ones not to put something in it for laughs. Even the honest ones concerned me whether they washed their hands before kneading the dough or something along those lines. I always accepted food and took it back to my office where it sat until the end of the day and then it always went out with the night trash.

Exceptions were made for food that Mrs. Jefferies made and sent with her kid. She did catering and I had never tasted pies and cookies as good as she baked. I had, on occasion, actually commissioned a couple dozen chocolate chip cookies or a pie for the weekend if it had been a while since I had seen any come across my desk at school. Fortunately, she had two sons. The one graduating this year and one that was a freshman, which meant I had enjoyed four years of culinary bliss and had three more years of goodies to look forward to. I wasn't too proud to be bribed and she wasn't too pious to try. We had a good relationship and the fact her kids' schedules got done first and they usually got the classes they wanted was nothing more than a coincidence since someone had to be first.

I was totally immersed in thoughts of pie when the bell rang and last Monday was off and running. As the students bounced and giggled their way towards class with a little extra excitement in their step, I slowly worked my way back towards the office. I stood outside the door until the tardy bell rang and the last student disappeared into a classroom. No one wanted to get that last tardy that would prevent them from being exempt from semester tests so they had it timed to the second.

I pushed through the door and greeted Ms. Shelly and Donna Clinton. Donna had been with us almost a week working as the attendance clerk and had made remarkable progress. Regina had been able to train Donna in two days and felt comfortable enough to go ahead and leave her with the job so she could go care for her ailing mom. Donna proved to be as bright as I had suspected and as far as I know, Ms. Shelly had only had to mention covering up her tattoos once and I noticed a blouse opened three buttons down one morning when she walked in that had been buttoned up two by the time I made it to the office. From the way I could hear them talking during the day, it seemed that Ms. Shelly and Donna had hit it off well despite Ms. Shelly misgivings. I suspected Donna would thrive in this environment and having a friend like Ms. Shelly couldn't help, but make life more enjoyable. I know having Ms. Shelly as my friend had made my life more enjoyable.

After exchanging good mornings and everyone shouting 'last Monday', including the nurse and a couple of office aides, I turned to go to my office to do a little graduation preparation. Donna shouted after me just before I got to my door, "Mr. Masters. I have a parent needing to speak to you. Is now a good time?" she asked across the office.

Okay so Donna hadn't learned everything and Ms. Shelly would have to teach her the 'parent rule', which is I didn't talk to parents unless I absolutely had to and then only as a last resort. The second is the 'currently busy' rule, where I always needed an excuse like I was in a meeting or had another parent already waiting on me or something like that.

To ask for the meeting right in front of the parent gave me no wiggle room and pretty much meant I had to see them. Since she was new, I would forgive Donna this time, that and the fact that she looked great. It was amazing what regular hours, some sleep, and healthy meals could to for someone that had all the pieces in place to begin with.

"Sure," I said much more cheerily than I felt. "What do we have this morning?"

"This is Mrs. Francie Murdoch and she has a question about her sons missing semester exams." Donna reported as she pointed to a lady sitting along the wall.

I smiled and walked towards her to introduce myself. "I'm William Masters, the principal. What can I do for you today, Mrs. Murdoch?" I said politely, once again sounding much more sincere than I really felt. All that was going through my mind was I'm five days away from graduation and parent conferences should have been over for this year.

Francie rose to her full height of somewhere close to four and half feet. She reached out a hand that was on the end of an arm that had a serpent tattoo that circled its way up and disappeared over her shoulder. Since Francie was wearing a spaghetti strap top, I was able to see the tail descending over her shoulder. With her other hand, she was trying to dig the hem of her very short shorts out of the creases of her thighs and her butt. Most of the material that made up the shorts was wedged somewhere so that most of her legs and a portion of what I assumed was leopard print underwear was visible. On her right leg was a tattoo of a Harley that ran the length of the outside in very detailed artwork. The text, which was clearly visible above the 'bitch seat' and just made it out from under the hem of her shorts, said 'Soft Tail'. Knowing motorcycles, I was aware that actually was the name of a model of Harley, but I wasn't really sure that was the reference. I figured it worked both ways. She was adorned with several piecing including a belly ring that was visible below the hem of her too short top. Her hair was bleached blonde and was pulled back with a red bandana and

71

the whole ensemble was completed with ankle high spiked leather boots.

As I took this all in, I was thinking there was not going to be any good to come out of this meeting even if she offered to dance naked on my desk, which I considered to be a very real possibility. I motioned for Francie to come on into my office where we could talk. As I passed Ms. Shelly, she refused to make eye contact, but I could see her smiling behind her computer monitor. She was going to enjoy this I knew.

"Francie, Ms. Clinton said you had a problem with semester tests?" I asked opening the conversation.

"No, what I have a problem with is that I need to leave town on Wednesday and take my boys, but not all of them are exempt and I need to find out what I can do about it. I have to leave town," she said in a very calm tone that sounded reasonable and non-threatening.

I thought that's a good start so let's see if I can keep from pissing her off. We have parents all the time wanting to get out of town for summer vacation a couple of days earlier than the school lets out. We could dismiss on February 16th and there would be a parent needing to leave on Valentine's Day for a wedding or something. This wasn't anything new so I wasn't worried.

"May I ask the nature of your trip and why it can't wait until Friday?" This was said in my most innocent tone trying to get information before I made any kind of decision.

When she got up and closed the door, the alarms in my head starting going off. I never shut the door when a girl or woman was in my office for my own protection and to make them feel a little more comfortable. Occasionally, when dealing with a female student over a private matter, Ms. Shelly or Mary Nell, the counselor would sit in. I was now inside the office with a woman barely dressed and whose appearance radiated provocative behavior. Hmm Hmm. Just when I though it was safe to go back into the water.

"I shut that door because it's not really anybody's business what I do or don't do, but since I'm here asking you for help, I guess you deserve to know. I'm a witness in a trial over in

72

Denton that starts on Wednesday and they aren't sure when I will be called so the lawyers said I had to be readily available. I'm actually the key witness in their case and I have to be there. I don't got any place to leave the boys, plus the lawyers are planning on putting us up in a hotel that has a pool and room service, which is the closest thing to a vacation these kids have ever had and I don't want them to miss it," Francie explained as if she was telling me about a recipe for apple pie she had found in Ladies Home Journal.

"Okay," I nodded thinking through the possibilities, which she must have mistaken for me needing more details.

"It's like this Mr. Masters. I was married to Luis, who was the twin's daddy. Oscar and Benny Garza. You know them?" she asked and I nodded recognizing for the first time which students we were talking about. Oscar and Benny were sophomores and didn't cause much trouble. Their grades weren't good, but they were passable. I saw them in the cafeteria regularly with several other boys and they seemed well adjusted. Okay, so Oscar and Benny Garza. I made a mental note.

She continued convinced I had Oscar and Benny pegged. "Well, Luis had been gone on the road a lot delivering goods up and down I-35 and was spending more and more time away from home. I think he had himself a little 'ho on the side over in Grand Prairie. Well I got tired of sleeping alone with my vibrator, so I started going out with Big Sugar who is Delphonso's dad. You know Delphonso right, Delphonso Johnson?"

"Yes, I know Delphonso. He's a sophomore right. Pretty tall kid. Needs to be playing basketball and eating more?" I said mostly to myself as I classified kids by their unique appearance or talents. "He's your son as well?" I asked starting to feel like this was slowly getting away from me.

"Well Delphonso isn't my biological son, but when the stabbing happened I took him in cause I felt sorry for him." Once again she described the events as if we were having coffee talking about the new deli in town. "See Big Sugar and I saw each other most nights when Luis was on the road and we had some good times. Someone must have told Luis cause one night when he was supposed to be in Waco, he came busting into the bedroom and caught Big Sugar and me in bed. I was just getting Big Sugar big when there was Luis yelling and screaming and waving a gun. Neither Sugar nor I knew what was happening at first since we had been focused on other things, but Sugar quickly realized we were in danger. The problem though was that Big Sugar was lying on his back across the bed and I was all astraddle of him and he couldn't move. Well, I guess with all this extra strength because Luis has a gun and all, Sugar just chunks me across the room into an open closet. I landed in a laundry basket and hit my head on the back wall, but was conscious enough to hear a couple of gunshots and then some scuffling and shouting. I managed to claw my way out of the closet just in time to see Sugar run Luis through with the blade Sugar carried in his boot. And that was it for Luis. So I have to testify for Big Sugar that he was only defending himself and me when he stabbed Luis. He's been awaiting trial for almost a year now and finally it starts on Wednesday," She said as if everything should now be perfectly clear.

I ran through a lot of options when searching for the most appropriate response and really couldn't put my finger on the best one so I just led with the traditional, "I really sorry for your loss."

"Luis?" she asked. "That weren't no loss. Don't be sorry about that lying, cheating piece of shit. He got what he deserved. I'm just missing Big Sugar something fierce though. It's been almost a year and I only cheat on him when I can't hold out any longer and none of those other guys mean anything. If they start getting serious, I tell them that Bug Sugar stabbed my last lover and I never see them again."

"Okay so let me look at the exemption list," I said as I scanned the names for Oscar, Benny, and Delphonso. After carefully checking twice, they were all three exempt after all. This was going to be easy. "Mrs. Murdoch, all your boys are actually exempt, so there's really no problem with you leaving on Wednesday. That's good news for all of us," I said relieved that this was solved and almost over. As interesting as the story had been and as entertaining as it was watching Francie as she adjusted her shorts and top on a regular basis trying to cover an acre of skin with a yard of cloth, I was ready for some normalcy to return to Last Monday.

"Harry's exempt? That little shit told me he had to take a test on Thursday and that was why I have been wasting your time. When I get a hold of him, I may just whack him good. I can't imagine why he wouldn't want to go stay in the hotel over in Denton and swim."

"Harry?" I asked. "Who's Harry?"

"Harry Murdoch. He's a sophomore and my first son by Luther Murdoch. Luther got himself blown up in a meth lab explosion right after Harry was born so I moved in with Luis. Luis and I had the twins the next year and thought life was grand for a while. I guess Luis got bored and started running around after all the good years I gave him until Big Sugar fixed that. Now I need to get Big Sugar out of the pen so we can all be a family again." She offered as a summary.

As I went back through the list and the records, Harry did indeed have a test on Thursday and based on what she had told me, if I kept my facts straight, was she had four boys all in the same grade. Harry had been retained one year and the twins and Delphonso were all the same age. Four boys, three dads, three nationalities, and a mom that led a life most of us couldn't imagine, but seemed to love her sons as much as any other mom I knew.

"Mrs. Murdoch, Francie. I think your circumstances warrant a special exemption. Harry wasn't lying since he does have a test on Thursday, but I can work with the teacher and allow you to leave for Denton and the trial. There won't be a need for him to make up the grade so you and the boys will be free for the summer. I hope it all works out," I said sincerely. I wanted her to find some semblance of stability for her boys before they were lost to the world of their fathers.

Francie got out of her chair, once again tugging at her shorts that had re-wedged themselves during our talk. She smiled and walked around my desk to shake my hand I supposed. She stopped short, standing directly in front of me and said. "Mr. Masters, I have a way to make men happy and I am very good at it. You have been so helpful to me this morning I'm willing to show you my gratitude." Her stance and hand placement made the message she was sending unmistakable and I sensed seeing her gratitude would be special.

I looked Francie up and down and saw no sign of malice or mischief present in her face. I got the feeling that Francie was grateful and she had her own way of showing her gratitude that had worked for her over the years. I also had the feeling she was very skilled and I would enjoy whatever she had in mind, but considering Big Sugar had stabbed her last lover he knew about and Ms. Shelly had a sharp letter opener in her desk drawer, I decided to take a pass.

"Francie, I appreciate the offer, but there's no need to thank me. I'm just glad I could help. I'll be curious how things turn out over in Denton and hope the boys like the pool and room service." I said as I stood and placed a hand on the tail portion of her dragon running down her back as I guided her to the door.

"Well you have been a great help. I'm so happy right now I could cry and if you ever change your mind, I work over at the V-Twins bar on the highway. My offer is always good." Francie said with a smile and a wink and walked out the door as her shorts became wedged again showing more of her bottom than should have been seen in school or any place else for that matter, but the butterfly tattooed that adorned her right butt cheek was colorful and well done I had to admit. I was brought out my reverie by the sound of Ms. Shelly clearing her throat a little louder each time until I turned to see what she needed.

"Are you through looking?" she asked.

"I'm just trying to decide if that was a Monarch butterfly or the Pearly Crescentspot. It's hard to tell them apart sometime." I said with as much seriousness as I could muster.

"I believe it's called a butt cheek and has no business fluttering around here. It could become an endangered species." Ms. Shelly responded with her own seriousness.

"Why I do believe you are right, but they are magnificent creatures are they not?" I finished with a smile and a wink for Ms. Shelly letting her know she was the one for me and that I knew she carried a letter opener in her desk.

II.

Having made one lady happy and one mad, I moved back towards the safety of my office to try and figure out the row assignments for graduation. For most other events, I had someone in charge and I showed up, gave a speech, or handed stuff out. Graduation was all mine. I considered it the grand finale of the year and of course for the seniors it was the end of their twelve, thirteen, maybe fourteen-year journey. I didn't want to take any chances of anything going wrong and if something did happen, then it was my fault and it was a lot easier taking the grief. I had yet to have a perfect graduation, but my goal was to do just that before I was through. Maybe this would be the year. I had fine-tuned and tweaked my plan, making adjustments each year and this really could be the year of perfection.

"William?" Ms. Shelly's voice came over the intercom.

"Yes, Ma'am," I answered without looking up from my drawing of rows and aisles on my legal tablet.

"Do you remember we have the send off this morning at ten?" She asked, knowing the answer.

"Oh yeah, the send off for the all-state band people right?" I covered my forgetfulness quickly with as much information as I could. "That's at ten?"

"Yes, sir. You have about two minutes until you dismiss the student body. Miss Alexander called and they have Lacy and Macy loaded along with their suitcases and clarinets. They can leave as soon as we are ready. She also said she got the map you drew for her and has it plugged into her GPS. She feels confident she won't get lost."

Miss Lucy Alexander was our first year band director. We got her straight out of the University at North Texas over in Denton and she was a top-notch musician. We brought her in to replace a legend that had been at Shasta High for over thirty years and finally decided it was time to call it quits. The three packs a day cigarette habit that had started to wear on his health and his weight nearing 300 pounds had a lot to do with his decision. Too many donuts and bus rides.

Lucy was excellent in her skills and knowledgeable about all aspects of directing a band. Her weaknesses came in experience working with kids and having absolutely no sense of direction. She quickly learned how to handle the kids, but was forever getting lost. Fortunately, after the first football game where the band wound up in Argyle forty-five minutes late, we got her a bus driver. The fact the football game was actually in Breckenridge was the biggest factor. When it was time to take our two state qualifiers to San Antonio, I offered to get her another sponsor to drive the minivan, but she was confident she could handle it and with just the two girls, it seemed like a waste of budget money to send another adult. The fact she worried about the districts money was another sign she was green. Most would have asked for two more sponsors and an extra night to rest up from the long drive.

As the time got closer, I sat down with her and drew her a map from Shasta to San Antonio and then to her hotel. Since the highway in front of the school led to the interstate, which led to San Antonio, it would be hard to get lost unless she pulled off for lunch and forgot how to get back on the freeway. That of course was a concern so I prepped Lacy and Macy to watch how they got off and to make sure they were going in the right direction after breaks. They said they could do that. I really felt like we were okay and now it was time for the big send off.

We had a tradition that any group or individual that made it to state got an all school send off. Sometimes it was a parade through the halls lined with kids and sometimes we lined the bus lane as they drove through in their bus or van. Either way it showed school spirit, gave all our students a peek at what could happen if they succeeded, and we all got to be part of the big event. With it being May and the morning bright and sunny, I opted for the outdoor bus lane send off.

The bus lane ran in front of school like a driveway for a Southern plantation. It had been added since Shasta High had been built over fifty years ago. I'm not sure they had busses back then, maybe they rode their horse to school and let them graze on the front lawn. Who knows? Sometime later they came in and scraped out a lane that led to the front stairs so students descended from busses and ran up the stairs into the school. Or walked, sometimes, shuffled into school.

The plan was to load Lacy and Macy in the faculty parking lot where the minivan was parked. Ms. Alexander would exit the parking lot, turn right, and pull the van through the bus lane to receive the cheers, whoops, and yells of the student body. As they exited the bus lane they would follow the access road until they could enter the highway and we all would go back to class. Simple. No room for error. Fool proof plan. I am the fool for thinking so.

As the student body lined the drive and the music from a boom box was cranked to the max, the energy built as the white minivan was seen moving toward the parking lot exit. As we all watched expectantly, the van took a left onto the access road and drove out of sight. I picked up my cell phone as I shook my head and dialed Lucy who I had put on speed dial and had her do the same for me. She answered on the third ring. "Hello."

"Lucy, weren't you going to come through the bus lane so the kids could give you a send off?" I asked

"I thought I was, but the lady on the GPS told me to take a left so I did?" she answered with the innocence of a child.

"The lady on the GPS?" I asked somewhat confused.

"I know what your map said, but the lady on the GPS said to turn left onto the access road and go to the end of the block and take another left and one more when I hit the road behind the school. She must be right because I am entering the highway right now and she said I had thirty miles until my next turn. I can do this I know. Thanks for everything Mr. Masters. We won't let you down will we girls? Better go now and focus on my driving." As I heard Lacy and Macy shout agreement in unison, she hung up.

I let the kids cheer and dance for a little while longer and then signaled for them to head back to class. Most of the students never noticed that the van didn't go past. They just assumed it had and they missed it. The few that even asked, I told them the truth. The van had to go get gas.

It's days like today that made me shake my head and smile. Nobody really was yelling at me, but people all around were making me laugh. What else could you do? I just hoped I saw Lacy and Macy again. If I got word the van was found in Mexico and the people and clarinets were missing, I might get concerned. Until then, happy trails. I loved my job.

III.

After another hour of uninterrupted work, I had graduation organized and the faculty memo sent out by email that let everyone know their assignment or duty during the ceremony. I'd had all the office time I wanted for while so I headed towards the cafeteria to check on Boomer. I hadn't heard from him all morning and he usually gave me the menu for the day, but nothing so far. I was afraid the seniors might have decided to prank him and tie him up somewhere. Not that I believed that could happen, but then I didn't believe most of the things that went on during my regular days as it was. As it turned out, he was leaning against one of the columns watching the kids eat without a care in the world.

"Hey Boomer, I hadn't heard the menu report and thought I had better come check on you. You alright?" I asked slapping him on the back.

"Sorry, Boss, I should have checked in, but when I saw it was turkey casserole, I knew better than to call you. I know how much you hate it and how much you hate seeing it sticking to the ceiling tiles and walls. I've been watching as close as possible and so far no one has started slinging it yet. I think they are just happy school's almost out, plus I told'em I was pulling their exemption if they flung food." Boomer reported in great detail.

"Turkey casserole! Seriously? Are they just cleaning out the refrigerators and dumping it all in a pot? They do know that some of these kids actually eat what's put on their tray don't they? Are there any health hazards involved here?" I asked incredulous at the behavior of my cafeteria ladies. Use it all, big or small, no morsel goes uncooked was their motto. I took comfort in the fact these kids filled their stomachs with all sorts of caffeine drinks and other junk food so they had to be immune to anything our cafeteria threw at them. Most of the students didn't bother eating. We had see sculptures of Jerry World, the Cowboys spacecraft looking football stadium, on tables made out

80

of casserole. An imitation of the Eiffel Tower was impressive and the best was probably Mount Rushmore. I gave prizes to the students for those creations trying to encourage the students to at least build with it so we could wipe it off tables. When it was flung on the ceiling or lobbed on the walls, it was harder to wipe up. Turkey casserole. Jeeez louise!

"Boomer, if you're okay, then I'm going to go grab a bite to eat and start looking at the last exemption list to post for tomorrow." I said needing to leave the din of the lunchroom.

"I'm good boss, the ladies in the back had a couple of chili dogs left over from last week so I had them and then I found a frozen pizza in one of the coolers they warmed up for me. I am good to go" He said with a satisfied look on his face and a little tomato sauce on his shirt. Maybe it was chili. Didn't matter.

I could tell Boomer had it under control so I walked towards the front door and my truck. I needed a break from this day even it was only for a cheeseburger and fries from the Dairy Whiz. I knew I was breaking my rule about showing up between eleven and one, but this close to the end of school, how many old farts could have questions about anything left in this school year? Old enough to know better is a term I remember from my mom since I was little. Evidently I had never reached that magical age.

Floyd started my way as soon as I slid into the vinyl booth next to the wall. I had placed my order, but hadn't yet gotten anything but my drink. I had hoped to get in and get out without having to do more than wave or give a 'how you doing, Bob'. Floyd was going to make sure that didn't happen. He slid in on the opposite side of the booth and managed to shove the table with his large belly so that my side of the table was tight against my stomach. I was starting to feel trapped by the table as well as his demeanor. He was not looking happy.

"How you doing, Floyd?" I asked as casually as I could hoping to get off on the right foot.

"Not so damn good, Billy. I still gots the same problem I had last fall that you was going to fix." He said through clenched teeth and more than a little accusatory.

I knew what Floyd's problem was before he sat down, because Floyd Hammershead, the most aptly named person on Earth, had the same problem on a regular basis and no amount of talking was going to get him to understand or let it go.

Floyd was a sixth generation dairy farmer and only one generation removed from the Neanderthals I'm quite sure. He was a few inches over six feet and his waistline probably measured close to his height. He had a head that would rival a boulder and his hat size had to be at least an eight and a half. Floyd owned a dairy at the edge of town adjacent to the school's Ag farm and he wore a pair of coveralls each day with rubber knee boots everywhere he went since he needed them in the cow lots in the morning and again in the afternoon. I guessed it was easier with his massive belly not to have to bend over to take them off. I sometimes wondered on hot days what kinds of gases were created in that self-contained environment where the temperature probably hovered slightly over one hundred degrees, a perfect incubator. I hoped I was never around to find out. Under his coveralls, Floyd wore a white crewneck t-shirt everyday except on Sundays when he wore a white long sleeve collared shirt his wife starched each week. His wardrobe saved a lot of decision making time I supposed and gave him more time to focus on his dairy operation and helping me run the school.

Whatever odors he may have produced from being around his cows all day or with his rubber boots didn't seem to affect his wife as they had produced fourteen children in about as many years as it took to squeeze them out one after another. Of course maybe she held her breath one time and was done with it for another nine months. I tried not to give it much thought, but a lot of the time when Floyd was rambling, my mind wandered to how the heck he and his wife were actually physically able to procreate once much less fourteen times. His wife was just shy of forty and looked sixty with all her life's juices drained out of her and he of course had all his juices and a lot of other peoples. Either she was a hell of an acrobat or Floyd here was hung like Balaam's ass. I usually had to wash my mind out with soap after a few of those thoughts.

Evidently, no one had explained to Floyd that the Agrarian Age had passed as had the Industrial Age, and since we were now in the Technology Age it wasn't necessary to grow your own workforce. With the technology available to farmers now, the cows practically milked themselves. Floyd's pride in the fact he and his boys ran the whole dairy operation by hand showed me more ignorance than anything. Either way, we had Hammershead kids out our ears on a regular basis and most of them inherited the intelligence of their sire. As a result, Floyd and I talked on a regular basis about one stupid thing I did after another and why all the teachers discriminated against his kids. I tried to listen and move on hoping he would finally let go, but between milkings, I guess he had plenty of time to think. Since he didn't have to spend that time on his wardrobe and his wife was probably pregnant or nursing, and his work force was cleaning the barns, he had time to focus on me.

When he wasn't ranting to me about his kids discipline reports or report cards, he complained to me about the stack of manure that was piled up at the Ag farm next to his fence and the flies he had to deal with. I was suspecting this conversation was going to be about manure so I got the ball rolling.

"Floyd, you know that Mr. Townsend cleared that pile of manure last October and spread it across your neighbors fields for fertilizer after we talked." I said reminding him that I hadn't ignored him.

"Well it damn sure is stacked up again with flies buzzing all around my house and I'm wondering why it stays that way until I call you," He stated with some indignation.

"Floyd, I don't know much about animals, but I do know those are show animals and the kids feed them real regular, which I assume means they poop on a regular basis as well. With the animals pooping and the kids mucking their stalls, we are going to get a pile of manure a couple of times year, but we always haul it off and you know that." I said with a little bit of assertiveness to let him know I wasn't interested in taking a licking today.

"You may think you haul it off regular like, but I'm the one that has to deal with the flies it attracts and I say it ain't regular enough. I got flies all over my place and can't even eat supper without holding a fork in one hand and a swatter in the other." He said demonstrating with imaginary utensils.

I kept looking at the counter to see if my food was ready hoping to have them bag it and I could get the hell out of here. Floyd had settled in nicely and the more he relaxed the tighter the table pushed against my stomach and pinned me to the back of the booth. I didn't want to rile Floyd too much because I knew he could belch and break my spine in half if he chose to, but I also didn't want to listen to his chronic bitching with graduation just five days away.

"Floyd how many milk cows do you and your kids run out at your place." I asked

He was temporarily caught off guard with the change in the line of questioning. Fooling Floyd was not hard, kind of like messing with a golden retriever, and could be done for amusement if one decided to. I wasn't doing it for amusement. He perked up with an opportunity to talk about his dairy.

"I have fifty cows we run in the barn twice a day. Me and my boys milk every last one of them by hand and carry the pails ourselves." He said with pride and a practiced delivery that indicated he spouted that information on a regular basis.

Once more I wondered why you would feel so good about living so far in the past, but if it made him happy and kept the boys busy, good for them.

"Those cows poop like other cows?" I asked innocent enough.

"Sure's hell they do. Half the time we are milking the other half is spent hosing down the barn and the walk-ups." He added enthusiastically.

"Then how can you tell that the flies that are after your cornbread and beans are my flies and not your own milk cow flies?" I said trying really hard to remain serious and not to smirk.

Once again there was confusion in his eyes having been talking about his operation and how proud he was and then I was back to flies and seemed to be insinuating the flies were his own. The confusion turned to a slow boil and I felt the table tighten around my waist as he drew in a breath and held it while his mind tried to figure out the proper response. So much for not pissing Floyd off, but fortunately, Celina behind the counter called my number. There was no way I was going to be able to get up and get it so I waved for her to bring it if she would. She slid a red tray with a large order of fries and a cheeseburger in front of me and asked if there would be anything else in what I felt was a somewhat sarcastic tone. When the heck did waiters stop waiting? I'd leave her a tip if that was what was needed. Couldn't she see I was pinned to the wall?

I slung the fries out on the tray and squeezed a large glob of catsup on the wrapper and poured salt profusely over them and dressed my burger much the same. Floyd was once again side tracked as he focused on the food in front of him helping himself to one fry after another. I didn't mind if it kept him happy. I just needed to be through before the fires ran out or he remembered I had trapped him just a minute ago.

"You got a sassy mouth!" Floyd said with fries stuffed in both cheeks. "That's the problem I have with you. Someone should have smacked you a few times when you were growing up and maybe you wouldn't be so sassy. None of my kids give lip and there's a damn good reason for it!" He showed me the backside of a hand that could have passed for a door on a '57 Buick. "First time any of 'um tries, this is the last thing they see until they wake up. Never have to tell'em twice. Maybe you need some smacking?" he asked as a question, but was really more a suggestion. Evidently the food had energized his brain cells. "What you fail to realize Billy is that you work for me! I'm a taxpayer and you are my employee." I held my tongue. "What I expect when I tell you to do something is that you will do it and if you don't, well then I need to fire your ass. I can have your job you know!" He was building steam and the table was cutting into my stomach making it hard for me to focus or breath.

I have suggested that people could have my job when they make that statement and offer them my keys and maybe tell them the next five functions they need to attend. I have suggested they wouldn't like my job if they took it because of all the assholes they'd have to put up with. A few that I outweighed, mostly women, I have suggested they couldn't handle my job. Not that they couldn't handle it because they were women, but I insult the smaller people that can't hit as hard as larger ones. Today wasn't a good day to go there. Big Floyd already wanted to backhand me for having a sassy mouth so I didn't need to give him a reason to actually do it. I had several options at this point. I could order more fries and hoped food helped, I could get up and walk away and only delay the conversation, or I could fire truck him. If I chose to fire truck him I had to sound sincere, but there would be a fine line between success and getting bitch slapped across the floor of the Dairy Whiz.

"Floyd you pay taxes right?" I asked

"Just said I did and that makes you work for me!" he slammed a fist onto the table

"School taxes I know, how about county taxes? You pay those?" I asked if I were having a serious fact finding discussion with Floyd.

"I pay all my bills and I pay them on time. I am a loyal American citizen and I do my part and I expect to get results in return." He could have saluted a flag as he responded and I wouldn't have been surprised.

"Ever been down to the fire station?" Keeping my questions short and my tone level.

Confusion showed briefly in his eyes again as I shifted away from the main topic.

"I been down there. Usually take a couple of my kids each summer when they are old enough. Kind of like a vacation. We go between milkings while the older boys are hosing down the barn." He shared once again proud of himself.

"They ever let you drive the fire truck?" I asked getting closer to thin ice and deep water.

"Naw, I never drove the truck, but they did let us ring the bell." He said with some thoughtfulness trying to remember, completely missing the point.

"Do you think they'd let you drive the truck if you asked?" thin ice was creaking as I crept closer to the edge.

"Hell, no. They wouldn't let just anyone drive the fire truck. That's for fires and those fireman have to be trained and all." He added with confidence.

Deep breath, soft voice, sliding to the edge of the booth in case I needed to leap away from being crushed, "If you pay taxes to

86

buy the fire truck, but don't expect to drive it because it's for highly trained individuals, then why in the hell do you expect to drive my school when its run by a highly trained individual? Your taxes says you get your house put out if its on fire and your fourteen kids get a free education, but no where do they guarantee that I work for you or you get to run my school! Now if you want to come by some day I will dang sure let you ring the bell, but that's as far as it goes. Got it?" I ended almost shouting hoping to get his attention and make sure he knew to quit messing with me. Hopefully logic worked in his brain sometime.

I waited for the anger and for the outburst. I even waited for the crushing blow that would snap my spine and put me out of this misery. None of it happened. It was eerie. All I saw was a smirk slide across Floyd's lips and he slowly bobbed his head up and down as he hummed slightly to himself. He eyed me for almost a minute before he spoke. It was more than a little frightening.

"Sassy mouth. Big college boy. Always the jokes. Hmmm hmmm," he said still nodding. "Well Mr. Smart mouth, I'm smarter than you think. I knew you wouldn't do nothing, but make fun of me and try and trick me so I tricked you first." His smile kept getting bigger and bigger. "Last night I went over to the Ag farm and took me one of those prize pigs. I'm holding it for ransom. Either that pile of shit is gone by the end of the week, or I'm having ham and eggs for the next two months!" and he let out a laugh most often heard in horror movies by the villain.

Now it was my turn to smile. First, because it was so comical thinking about him sneaking commando style into the Ag barn and wrestling a pig back under the fence into his dairy barn. The mental imagine would be worth a laugh for months if not years. Second, I had to give it to ol' Floyd. He was always thinking. He just never end up with the right conclusion.

"Floyd, I need you to listen to me and understand I'm not messing with you anymore okay? We've had our differences, but I believe you are always sincere if not most times misguided, but this time you screwed up big time." I was sincere and wanted to get through to Floyd.

"Running scared now college boy. Have you over a barrel? Where's your sassy mouth now?" he taunted as I thought, crap, Floyd, you ignorant moron.

"You're playing chicken with a pig, Floyd!" I said with a lot more urgency. I needed Floyd to wake up.

"There's that sassy mouth. Trying to be funny, huh. Not going to work this time. I got the goods and you can't have them. I'm thinking smoked bacon for breakfast and ham for supper until I can't eat it no more. That there pig I took is big enough to feed all us for a while." He said with a lot of satisfaction.

I let him gloat until I thought he might be ready to listen and then I asked, "Who do you think owns those pigs?"

"That's the school barn so those would be school pigs. How dumb do you think I am?" he asked answering his own question.

"Floyd those are show pigs, goats and steers. They cost thousands of dollars and they are shown by students at fairs all over Texas and then sold for enough money to send them to college." I explained

"So I'm going to be eating really expensive bacon is what you are telling me. Stuff the president eats? And those Arab sheets." He was still grinning, not seeing the train barreling down the track right for him or having an understanding that the sheiks weren't called that because of what they wore and didn't eat pigs.

"No Floyd, what I'm telling you is those animals don't belong to me or the school. They are purchased by the parents for their kids to show. Those parents are some of the more prominent members of our community that have thousands of dollars tied up in one animal. One of those parents, I suspect, holds the note to your farm and more than likely is the owner of that pig you took. So what I am telling you is that if that pig goes missing, either you are going to lose your dairy or wind up in jail charged with felony theft. Or both!" I stated firmly looking Floyd straight in the eye trying to get him to understand this was God's honest truth with no sassy to it.

For a few seconds the grin still lingered on his lips and his mind played over and over how he had outwitted the sassy mouth prick once and for all and then as if his resistance were

88

like a snowman on a very hot day, it began to melt away as reality crept in. His face fell and panic replaced his jubilation. I reached over with my hand and actually patted the big bear paws that were now pressed together as if in prayer.

"I can help you, Floyd." I said calmly hoping not spook him. If he bolted and ran, we might have had a hostage situation on our hands. I couldn't see anyone wanting to try and pry him out of his house.

"What have I done? I can't lose my farm. I have kids to feed and my boys need jobs. I can't lose it. I have lived there my whole life." Floyd was starting to panic and he was rambling now.

"I can help you Floyd." I said again as calmly as I could. Her turned this time and looked almost pleadingly into my eyes.

"Listen very carefully, okay?" he nodded. "Go home and load the pig up in a trailer and pull it back over to the Ag farm. I'm going to call Mr. Townsend to meet you out there. As far as we know, the pig got loose and ran over to your house and you are just returning it like any good citizen would. Okay? Got it. It got loose. You're returning it. You want to do the right thing." I kept trying to put thoughts into his head for later in case he got flustered, they would come back to him. He just kept nodding with a blank look on his face.

I picked up my cell phone and dialed the school office and asked Ms. Shelly to put me through to Mr. Townsend. She asked if I was enjoying my extra long lunch and did I have any plans to come back to work today. I said 'Floyd Hammershead' and she said 'oh, sorry' and put me through. After explaining to Mr. Townsend how one of the pigs had gotten out and Floyd wanted to return it, Mr. Townsend agreed to meet him out at the Ag farm in an hour to re-pen it for him. He was confused as how a pig could have escaped, but was awful grateful Floyd was the one that found it. It was worth several thousand dollars he said. He would have to talk to the kids again about checking their gates each night before they left. Silly kids. I hung up and turned to Floyd.

"I'm fixing to make you a hero and you might even get a reward. I'm also going to have a dump truck out at the farm next

89

Monday after graduation to haul the shit off. In return you are going to quit busting my balls and eating my French fries, okay?" I asked with a half smile as I slid out of the booth and started my exit, still not sure as to Floyd's mental state.

Floyd rose to his full height and girth, looked me squarely in the eye, and said, "Sassy mouth boy." But he then took me between his bear paw hands and gave me a hug that reminded me of being behind the table a few minutes ago only this time I couldn't breath at all. Fortunately, it stopped short of me turning blue. He set me back down on the floor and walked out without another word. I didn't figure Floyd could last long without bitching about something, but maybe today we made a breakthrough. Maybe I'd let him drive the fire truck if I ever got one.

IV.

I drove back into the school parking lot listening to a Beatles CD. Hearing John Lennon singing 'All you need is love...' made me think even the largest beast in the form of a Floyd Hammershead could use a little love sometime. I didn't want to make it a habit since people might start thinking I was going soft and take advantage of me. 'Last Monday' had been like the carnival that came through town once a year and I had spent all my tickets on the rollercoaster. The ups and downs were making me nauseous and I was thinking it needed to stop soon or I might lose the little bit of the lunch I manage to keep away from Floyd. I had passed on a sexual escapade with Francie that I am sure would have rivaled anything I might find on late night pay per view and then sidestepped being turned into a human vegetable by a man that could have done it easily. A day in the life...I loved my job.

Ms. Shelly smiled when I strolled back in humming *Cocaine Blues* by Johnny Cash. She asked me once before why I spent so much time singing a song about man that shot his woman down. I insisted it was a song of redemption because in the end the message is lay off booze and drugs. She didn't buy it. Mainly it's a catchy tune that gets stuck in my head and shake frees when my mind was preoccupied by other things. I sang a lot of Johnny

Cash since even I can sing that well. I actually did a pretty good imitation when I tried.

As I passed her desk on my way to what I hoped was a peaceful sanctuary inside my office, she handed me a piece of paper. I stopped to see what it was and looked up to see her focusing on her computer screen trying very hard to contain her laughter. Evidently she had shared the joke with Donna, who now seemed to be one of her best friends, and they both burst out laughing as they watched my face turn red.

Bitty Snodgrass, or as I like to refer to her as Old Biddy, sometimes Damn it Bitty, and mostly that dang heifer, was my English Department Head. She knew the English language forward and backwards since she probably wrote the stuff to start with and was constantly correcting my grammar and many times had sent back memos with red markings on them for each mistake I had made. She had never gone as far as to give me a grade, but on one she felt was extremely atrocious, she had made a sad face.

I had tried very hard to be understanding, but over the years it had grated on every nerve I had and finally I had confronted her about it. It was like yelling at your sweet little grandmother with her lace collar and rimless glasses. I'm sure she had knitting under her desk to work on during her conference period. Her age was somewhere between 75 and ancient since she had reached the stage of white hair, and pale, powdered, translucent skin that refused to divulge a woman's age after say 70. Her face was constantly fixed with a smile as sweet as the angels themselves.

I had a full head of steam when I entered her room and had every intention of telling her to kiss my ass. My job was to communicate and did she understand the content of the memo and if so that was all that was important. I didn't need nor want anymore of her red pen critiquing of my writings. Instead, looking into her clear blue eyes and seeing Mother Mary herself, I started off as kindly as I could. Half way through my opening sentence she corrected part of my speech and then explained how she wanted me to be the best I could possibly be and how my writings were read far and wide so they needed to reflect the intelligence she could see I possessed. She wanted others to know the kind of man she got to work for and hoped she could do her part to make me the man I was capable of being. Then she gave me a cookie and I'm not sure, but I think she patted my bottom and sent me on my way.

When I got back to my office I was fuming. I had been had. I knew that angelic face was a façade and she had to be Lucifer incarnate. That sweet little old lady act may have won this time, but she wasn't going to fool me again. No she wasn't! I just never had gotten up the nerve to go back into her room alone again. So when she sends my memos back I just seethed and kept going. Every time I wrote anything for public view now, I spent extra time writing and rewriting just to take away her evil pleasure. I know what you're thinking, that she was actually making me better. Well, if that's what you wanted to believe then go ahead and fall under her innocent old lady spell. It's pure evil and I refused to give her the satisfaction of red lining me. I knew dang well that if we peeled off the rubber mask, I'm sure she wore, underneath would be the face of Lucifer himself.

The memo today was written while I was still thinking about Francie, her Soft Tail, and those leopard print panties. My imagination had a lot to work with as far as her special skill set and I had pushed my creative powers to the limit already this afternoon. It caused me to be a little sloppy on the graduation memo and now I was paying the price. I had done this job long enough to appreciate karma, yin and yang, voodoo stuff. If good came my way, I knew it would be balanced by bad and vice versa. I never get too excited about what looks like the winning lottery ticket kind of happenings, but then again it keeps me from getting too worked up about the end of the world kind of things either. Karma. Voodoo. The Big Bu.

Francie was a good thing. The gods of fate sent me a looker that had a problem I could fix and she felt indebted. Plus the butterfly on her butt I swear fluttered when she walked. I had my share of evil thoughts about most of that and in return, I got spanked by Floyd at the Dairy Whiz. But since I wound up doing him a favor and keeping him out of jail, I must have negated part of the bad, so the old heifer had to balance the books. I knew how it worked so I crumpled up the paper and stalked into my office to take my medicine leaving Shelly and Donna laughing hard enough to cry.

After a few minutes of deep breathing I had almost regained my normal blood pressure when Ms. Shelly appeared in my doorway.

"William, with all that you had going today, I just wanted to make sure you remembered this afternoon we let out early so the district can have its employee awards assembly." She stated softly I suspect hoping to make it easier to take. It didn't' work.

I just looked at her, shook my head and slowly repeated, "Holy crap. Damn, Damn, Damn!"

"It's just an hour you know and then you can have a beer and watch the Rangers. Who do they play tonight? Chicago?" she asked trying to distract.

"Damn a mighty, gosh a' Friday! No, they're on the road against Oakland so the game won't start until 9. It's just an hour with Sylvia Benson and listening to Super Dan drivel and gush over the other campuses like we are the ugly stepsisters is the last thing I need after today. Last Monday, why did you forsake me?" I whined and pouted.

"You done?" she asked like a mother waiting for the temper tantrum to be over so the scolding could commence.

"Yes ma'am," I said, chastised.

"You got five minutes until you need to dismiss everyone and send the adults to the auditorium," she reminded me as she turned and left.

V.

Every school district I imagine had some sort of end of year bash. It was a necessary assembly to pass out time of service five-year pins, ten-year pins, and so on. It was also a time to recognize the retirees and give the education version of the gold watch- a plastic cube with the school crest on it. All of this was mixed in with Super Dan's year in review speech and Sylvia Benson coordinated all this.

Sylvia is our Director of Curriculum/HR person. As far as I could tell she handled the Convocation at the beginning of the year, the end of year awards assembly, and the faculty Christmas party. Other than that I honestly didn't know what she did since she had a secretary to handle the HR paperwork. Super Dan brought her in a few years ago from a school near Austin with big fanfare regarding her expertise in raising test scores and being the answer Shasta needed for academic advancement. In the five years she had been here, I could honestly say she had been on my campus twice so if she was impacting high school curriculum, it had to be distance learning for my teachers. Her background was elementary so I suspect she was afraid of us.

Sylvia wasn't a bad person and I had more than one conversation with her over the years. She was just in way over her head. She was a cliché. A person that had scaled the ladder to stardom with a skill set unrelated to the job responsibilities. This happens in many vocations I'm sure, but education lends itself to it more than say rocket science where the first explosion usually brings about termination in every sense of the word.

Sylvia had ascended the leadership ladder on her good looks and charm and over the years had maintained her position using smoke and mirrors. Actually, it was designer clothes and cleavage that kept her afloat. She was talented and the fact she was still out front carrying on spoke volumes of her God given talent. Well God gave her the framework and the talent was applied by some very skilled medical craftsmen. I felt they had created a masterpiece honestly.

After observing Sylvia for five years I was able to dissect her approach and realized how smart she was. Some where along the line she realized she was going to drown if she didn't learn to swim so instead of having to learn curriculum, she realized she could buy designer clothes and have a connection with the women. Anytime someone came up to her or ask a question, she commented on their clothes, which invited a comment back about hers, which were always the latest design. That opened the door and she spent the next few minutes discussing clothes before having to rush off to places unknown for consultation on who knows what. She had endeared herself to the more prominent female faculty members by having a 'garage sale' by invitation only, in her closet. Some of her outfits were seen in

94

the classrooms regularly now. You would notice had you paid attention. She chose her allies well.

Guys. We were easy. She was over forty, dressed thirty, and acted twenty. Her blouses were all low cut and her hems rode high on her thigh. If a guy wanted to take a peek, she wasn't opposed; after all she was a masterpiece that was created for viewing. Guys rarely think about curriculum anyway so most men approached her for the pleasure of her company. She was pleasant company no doubt. She was aware that her boss was a guy and six of the board members were guys and she made sure she stood close enough they could feel her presence and each got a pat on the hand or a touch to the face whenever she stopped by before board meetings 'just to say hi'.

Margaret, the only female board member was always given a special comment about her wardrobe, which could best be described as Flower child meets Wall Street. Margret could pay for the medical miracles Sylvia had commissioned with the cash in her purse and wasn't the least bit fooled by Sylvia's act. When the time came that Sylvia became detrimental to the kids, Margaret would have her on the next bus out of town. Right now Sylvia actually served a purpose. Too bad her title wasn't district hostess, because then it would be an accurate reflection of her job. She did throw a hell'uva party.

The fact that curriculum is kind of important in a district and most places look to the director for answers was the downside to having a public hostess and the only school owned margarita machine in the state, but fortunately, I had spent enough time as a teacher to be aware of what was needed and stayed up to date. My faculty was solid and we did the job well. Most times that's all it took, a little dedicated interest.

When the kids were out of the building and Boomer had the bus riders wrangled, I went down to the auditorium to be visible during the assembly. Shasta High was built over fifty years ago and the auditorium reflected the times. We could have staged a performance of the Phantom of the Opera and seated most of the people in Shasta as well as the surrounding county. Our auditorium was used for every event that required more seating than the First Baptist Church and rarely was it filled. The entire

95

faculty and staff of Shasta ISD sat up towards the front and didn't come close to filling it half full. As usual, most of the coaches were scattered to the rear of the rest of the staff. I sat on the back row myself in case I had to handle an emergency or something, a habit I picked up in church.

Most folks had gotten their juice and cookies, provided as a sugar rush to keep everyone alert for a few more minutes, and were finding their seat. Teachers at the end of a workday, seated in a darkened area, had a tendency to doze since many hadn't slept a full night since last August. Sylvia probably needed to require everyone to eat a minimum of two cookies. Since they were Mrs. Jefferies', I had taken four myself since everyone had been given first chance at them. No use having them go to waste and if I'm lucky and there still some left after this is over, I'll have dessert tonight!

All the while a power point of school year activities were playing on the large screen above the stage. I had time to watch it through once before the program started and if I counted correctly, and I did since it wasn't hard, there were exactly three pictures from the high school. One was a shot of the front of the building that Sylvia must have taken from the curb a quarter mile away, two were pictures of football games, both of which we lost, that had appeared in the Shasta Daily News, and she must have borrowed them. The rest of the presentation, of course, was mainly the elementary kids and all their cutesy faces, glue, and colored pictures. A few from the junior high showed the amazing transformation that happened when hormones began racing through your body and it was not pretty.

No one should have to work with junior high kids. They were big enough to hurt you and not smart enough to know better. They were aggressive little punks that hugged their friends one minute and kicked them in the shin the next. The boys were even worse. From sixth grade to ninth grade, kids should be isolated and housed off somewhere and only be allowed to return when they were seasoned and ready to go to high school. I don't know who would watch them though is the only problem. Their own parents don't seem to like them very much either.

In a few minutes we would listen to Super Dan praise the little kids and tell us for the thousandth time how much he loved walking the halls and being around them. He spent more time over in Brenda McGillis' office, the elementary principal, than his own. They had been fast friends for years and spent a lot of time together. Just stating the facts. In her prime, Brenda probably was a hot little number and having a connection with the seat of power didn't hurt her career. She was good, no doubt. She had her scores at the top each year and was always the highest performing campus in our district. Her kids came everyday and those that didn't, woke up to find Mrs. McGillis standing at the end of their bed with her eyebrow arched. Her attendance ran above 99% regularly. She was good, but she also never had to fret over staff, funds, or equipment. If there was cutting that needed to be done, it wasn't from her campus. That was understood. It was nice to have connections. Bottom line, I like the little kids too. They were like puppies, funny to watch as they scampered around in their miniature adult bodies and their goofy faces. I just never was sure I could work where I had two kids wrapped around my legs like ankle weights as I made my way down the hall. I'm thinking I would rather have a thug tell me 'Hell no, dude' and walk out as opposed to having tears and snot on my shirt. I guess we all had our calling. I thank God he didn't assign me junior high chromosomes when he was creating my DNA.

As I ate my cookies and waited for what surely would be an hour of entertainment, I heard that familiar breathing again. That rhythmic kind that is easily recognizable. I turned toward the sound booth and my first thought was Joe Bob, you seemed to be improving with practice. Way to go dude. My second thought was, I hoped Chastity wasn't a screamer and if she was, I really needed her to time her 'Oh yes, Oh yes' with the announcing of the retirees names. Poor kids. I guess they saw an empty school with the entire staff in a meeting, what better time to get in a little bonding before they went their separate ways. Good news was they only had one more week and then they were out of here to live happily ever after I hoped.

People thought it nice how both had been awarded music scholarships to Ouachita Baptist University in Arkadelphia, Arkansas. How sweet, they said, that they would have each other to lean on as they went so far away from home and amazed that not one, but two of our students had chosen to go there. I, of course, knew they had been doing more than leaning on each other and far from home was the plan from the beginning. I thank Mary Nell McKenzie for helping them locate some scholarship money so they could at least eat more than once a day. I didn't have the heart to interrupt again and was beginning to feel like a peeping Tom or maybe a listening Tom so I moved a few rows forward out of earshot unless Joe Bob had really been studying and Chastity broke out into the Hallelujah Chorus.

A spotlight hit the stage and as the music that had been accompanying the slide show increased in volume, Sylvia Benson strode to the front and center of the stage to the applause of the crowd. After a short time acknowledging the adulation, the music subsided.

"Howdy!" Sylvia shouted sounding an awful lot like Minnie Pearl. She had used that line every time she spoke as if to assure the audience that even though she had been born in New Jersey, she had made her way to Texas as fast as she could and had studied the language along the way.

The crowd shouted various responses to which she held her hand to her ear signaling, 'I can't hear you!' In turn the crowd responded even louder, led by her hand picked posse, much to her satisfaction.

I smiled and then laughed to myself. I couldn't help it when I looked at the outfit Sylvia had on today. I am sure in her mind she was a Texas cowgirl. Maybe she even sent off for an authentic Dale Evans get up. She had the white felt hat, the silky blouse with plenty of cleavage so it couldn't be Dale Evans, and fringe. Her skirt was short, of course, and looked like the skirts the elementary kids like to wear so they could twirl and have it stand straight out. This all was accented by mid calf white boots.

What I saw was something similar to what the Dallas Cowboy cheerleaders had worn for the game against Philadelphia last fall to try and outshine the Eagles' spandex girls. The cheerleaders

I'm sure had spanks under theirs, but my money said Sylvia had no such thing. I do know that no one had ever told her that short skirts become even shorter on stage and the board members sitting the front row had a pretty good view of her talents. Then again knowing Sylvia like I did, she knew exactly where the board would be sitting, having placed the placards herself, and she also knew that they probably had just extended her contact and given her a rise or raise one when she twirled to show off her fashion statement. She wasn't worried about Margaret as long as it was 6-1 in her favor. She added a twirl for good measure.

After giving a rousing speech describing the spectacular achievement of Shasta ISD over the course of the last school year and praising the brilliant leadership of our Board and Superintendent, she turned the microphone over to Super Dan. Where Sylvia used her looks and charm to work her magic, Dan used his physically imposing size and bluster to bully his way through any problem. When it came time for him to speak to groups such as this he many times rambled since he refused to use notes and liked to be spontaneous to much to write a speech. The problem is that he always wound up saying basically the same thing or telling the same story because he reverted back to his few favorite memories.

Super Dan had at times referenced people and events in his speeches that had taken place long before I arrived and from the looks on people's faces around me, they had no clue either. Fortunately, his ego led him to believe a few rousing words from him was enough for anyone and he usually was done in less than five minutes. But not before we heard how much he loved the little elementary kids and how he was just over there today, and yesterday and the day before had he chosen to mention that.

Sylvia retook the spotlight and as service pins were passed out, people entertained themselves counting how many times she twirled her skirt in front of the board and how many time she adjusted her hat which had to be cramping her style. After the last award and retiree had been recognized, Sylvia informed us she had one last special award. I wasn't surprised when she asked Super Dan to come back to the front. I was just hoping she wasn't going to make us watch if she tried to jump him right there on stage. I was surprised when she awarded him a plaque for forty-five years of service. Forty-five years in the same district. How much whiskey would one have to drink to work in the same district for forty-five years?

I had traveled across the state and worked in several districts during my career. I found there were two kinds of people. The nomads like me that worked a few years and moved on out of boredom or for a promotion or better pay. Then there were the local yokels. The ones that most likely grew up in a town, went off to school, and came back to spend their entire life working in the school they had graduated from. Its kind of like being cut out for a certain grade level, it had to be in our DNA. Where I could see the locals having the sense of stability and knowing everyone in town and all their secrets, I think I would go stark raving mad from the tedium and boredom. I had been in Shasta twelve years now and that was a new record for me. Maybe this was going to be my final stop. Maybe Sylvia would give me a plaque when I had been here forty-five years. She could then gum me with her dentures and wheel me out in my wheel chair. Wasn't going to happen. I hoped.

The show ended and everyone fled for their cars with the knowledge that there were only four school days left. I was courteous enough to stop by and congratulate Sylvia on another smashing performance and encouraged her to come over more often, that we were good people, and she might like us. She smiled, took my hand and thanked me as she slid up close enough that I felt one of her professional grade boobs mash against my arm. Sylvia said she appreciated the job I did as she leaned in while looking at her watch to give me the opportunity for a peek if I was inclined. A practiced move no less skillful that an arabesque in ballet and I am sure as many hours had been used to perfect it. I just wondered to myself how really good she could have been had she only applied her efforts toward education. Oh well, I took my peek, thank her silently, and moved away knowing my time was over. I grabbed up four more cookies as they were clearing the platters and started for my truck.

100

Last Monday had been a tug of war and I felt like the rope. I slid in my Jack Johnson CD in the slot and as *You and Your Heart* flooded my ears, I couldn't help but think of the islands and I swear I could smell the ocean. As I drove towards Skeeter's to pick up a pail of his crispy fried chicken and cream gravy for supper, I once again added up the victories and subtracted the losses and declared my self the winner for today. I patted myself on the back. Winning. One day at a time. One year at a time. That's what it's all about.

Monday night was Ms. Shelly's book club night and she'd already left when I passed back through the office. Monday's usually meant take out chicken and a ballgame for me. The only variation was what season it was. Tonight it would be baseball and the Rangers were on the west coast. Late starting game. I already knew that with a bucket of chicken and a few beers, I would be sound asleep in my recliner long before the first pitch was thrown. I was convinced I would be watching the game, but odds were I would wake up around midnight and shuffle up the stairs to bed. Graduation t-minus four and counting!

Graduation

I.

The last Saturday in May is a holy day as far as I was concerned. Graduation day was the day that I started planning for 364 days in advance. I did give myself one day of solitude, to savor and relish the feeling of completion each year after the ceremony was over before I start mentally preparing and planning for the next one. I had actually written my next graduation speech in June of the preceding year although that's not the norm. Sometimes I was writing the last paragraph the night before. So far I had always managed to finish before it was time to actually give it.

The reason for the special attention was that in my eyes this was my final exam each year. It represented the whole year and how it went said a lot about how I felt the year went. The good news was that about the only person that held it in such high esteem and used it to gauge an entire year was me. The way I saw it, the graduation ceremony was the culmination of a student's entire academic life and what was possibly the only ceremony their parents and family would attend. Even if they went to college, a lot of students either skipped the ceremony or got lost in the masses. High school graduation was the one public acknowledgement that a student had successfully completed his or her requirements and could choose what they wished to do. And in my eyes the ceremony was for the parents.

I said this to each group of seniors when we sat down to discuss the ceremony and usually got some boos or other snotty comments, but I explained that for most of them, their parents were the ones that deserved a good show for all the hours they had spent hauling kids here and there, or getting them up, or helping with homework. Most of that was done early on and many had forgotten since they had their own ride or had pretty much kept their parents out of most of their lives. Unfortunately, more and more were becoming the exception, having to raise themselves and finishing in spite of the parents. But I wanted to put on a show that honored the parents or guardians while honoring the kids as well.

I got a lot of ribbing from friends and peers, because for the most part I was pretty flexible and had pretty wide standards when it came to running the school. I had been criticized as being liberal in my thinking and I usually cut kids a break when I could. But when it came to graduation I was the most conservative hardliner that had existed. I supposed it had to do with my passion for tradition and what it represented. I felt the kids didn't truly appreciate the moment and somebody had to do it for them so down the road they would be glad their picture was something they could share and not a freaky cartoon of some goof ball acting like on ass.

I refused to slack off on how they wore their caps and gowns. We didn't decorate or wear pictures on the tops of our caps like some of the kids shown in the Fort Worth Star Telegram from some of the larger Metroplex schools each year. Colleges had made graduation almost a costume party and I had a bigger battle each year holding the line, but as long as I was breathing, it would be my way or the highway. I felt good about the fact that the ceremony was just that, a ceremony and therefore it was optional. If a kiddo didn't want to behave or go along, I didn't get upset, I just told'em to drop by the office next week and pick up their diploma and have a nice life. BUT, if they intended to be part of their graduation, it would be by the guidelines I had. Most were willing to give me one more hour and honestly most wanted their parents to be proud. They usually found a way to get back at me anyway, but as long as on the surface all looked good, then I'm happy. One day I would pull off the perfect graduation, but until then, I would keep planning and preparing to get it right.

One of the major adjustments I had made over the years was practice. It used to be mandatory that ever student attended a practice session the day before. We would actually go through the entire ritual with the exception of the actual speeches. I wanted them to see every step needed and be prepared to execute on command. I was an idiot. It was like giving the enemy the plans for your sneak attack. They knew your every move and had twenty-four hours to prepare a counter attack. When I finally realized what was happening, I changed the whole approach. I practiced the teachers.

Starting a few years ago I developed the line leader approach. I assigned a teacher to each row of seats and taught them the process, how to march in, when to stand, when to sit, when to take their row to the front to get diplomas. The students had to watch their line leader who in turn communicated what was necessary at that given time. The students were like sheep. They had no idea what was happening and were dependent on paying attention to their leader or get left out or be embarrassed. By the time the students started feeling comfortable, the ceremony was over, and their celebration and juvenile behavior took place outside. My first step towards perfection!

Of course there were always kinks to every system and the line leader system had its own problems over the years. The biggest problem was a few of the teachers didn't pay any better attention to instructions than the kids did. I had line leaders that had gotten their kids through the door and then stepped aside and let them go into the auditorium on their on and after that of course they were literally lost as sheep. I had some leaders not think there were enough chairs so they had part of their row move to the next aisle, which of course screws up the whole alphabet thing. So over the years I began to identify reliable trust worthy leaders and find other jobs for the more creative airhead sorts.

Since my faculty was fairly stable and my numbers each year were about the same, I now had veteran line leaders that probably could walk through the entire ceremony without me saying a word. So that was a plus. But just in case, when I had so much confusion with the faculty, I implemented the name card step. Every student now had their name written on a piece of paper and when they made it to the announcer located on the edge of the stage, they handed it to them and were announced. Previously, working off a preprinted list, we had mad scrambling going on trying to get a kid up from the back of the line because his name was called and his line leader had brought them up backwards. Now, we sometimes do S's before the M's and one year I was listening and hearing W's thinking we were almost through and lo and behold they had gotten ahead of the H's. I never did figure that one out. But with the name cards, we don't care when they reached the stage, the name called was the one that was fixing to walk across the stage and hopefully the parents were paying attention and had their cameras ready.

Like most parts of the ceremony, if you didn't know what it was supposed to look like, it all looked good. So just like the students, the parents weren't sure who was supposed to walk where or exit which side of the stage, but when you had spent year perfecting the steps and you see the third smartest girl in the class come up to do the invocation and walk off the wrong way even though you had just coached them just minutes before, a small pain began to start in my stomach.

The next two steps to perfection that fell into place were the starting time and the diplomas. Having experimented with every possible start time, the perfect one was ten A. M. Saturday morning. No one yelled at you because the cousins or grandmas couldn't get off work in time to drive in for little Johnny's ceremony and he was the first Schuster to ever finish high school and everyone wanted to see it. It also allowed enough time for everyone to wake up and get to the auditorium, but didn't allow any time for drinking, partying, or screwing around like happened when it was at night. A little breakfast, maybe, mostly sleepy eyed students, no need for the breathalyzers, and grandma was there to see it.

As far as the diplomas, the only thing the kids got during the ceremony were the covers. Inside it was as blank as some of their minds on graduation day. This served two purposes. If they got out of line we didn't mix up the diplomas and have to chase kids down afterwards to swap. Second, and most importantly, I told them if they screwed up my show I would burn their diploma in the trashcan in my office. I had yet to do it, and wouldn't even if I wanted to, but the closest I came was when one of the 'mean girls', during our early years at Shasta, snuck her bedazzled cap into the auditorium and was only steps away from making it onto the floor when she walked under Boomer.

He yanked the sequined cap off her head and pulled her out of line to change hats and she called him an asshole. Fortunately, Boomer is a trained professional and simply slapped a spare cap on her head rather firmly and sent her on her way sulking as she walked. When she came up to school on Monday to get her diploma with the rest of the students, I let Boomer have the pleasure of lighting a piece of cardstock that looked exactly like a diploma after she refused to apologize to him. He held the match long enough to give her one last chance and she refused to blink so he lit the paper and watched it burn. Tears came through the glare of hatred as she saw her whole 12 years of education go up in smoke. She turned and stomped out still refusing to budge. It was about five minutes before the mom hit the front door of the school hysterical.

The good news was she wanted to know what she could do to fix it. I explained what had happened, what we asked her daughter to do, and all we needed was an apology to get her diploma. The mom offered an apology to Boomer and I informed her that wouldn't work since it needed to come from the daughter. Her mom explained the girl had always been a little stubborn and hard headed. I assured the mom that the girl's life was fixing to be a lot more difficult it she didn't learn to work with others and be willing to admit mistakes. When the mom asked once again if she could do the apologizing, I shook my head because the problem was obviously deeper than I could fix at this point. I made the mom swear she would make the girl apologize to her and then gave the mom her daughter's diploma. I figured she deserved something for living with Regan MacNeil, the Linda Blair character in the Exorcist. I'm pretty sure her head would have spun around if we had tried to force her to say the words 'I'm sorry'.

And the final step is location. I know a lot of the schools close to Denton had their gradation ceremony at the Coliseum on the campus of North Texas University. It was a nice venue and the school took care of most of the arrangements. It also provided plenty of seating. For large schools it was ideal, but having seen one of the smaller school's graduations, it was like working in a cavern and the whole ceremony was overshadowed by the fact everyone appeared like ants at a picnic. With our auditorium constructed in the early 20th century, we could still seat our kids and their families. If Shasta began to grow, there might be a problem, or God forbid they actually passed a bond election and built a new school, the auditorium would be much smaller and different steps would have to be taken.

In a pinch, the football stadium could be used and we had tried it several times over the years with weather rarely a factor once we moved it to morning. I moved away from even considering the stadium completely the year the maintenance department brought in cow manure and spread it around over the field for fertilizer the day before graduation. With no time to adjust and with all plans and invitations pointing towards the stadium, a giant plastic tarp was found and spread under the chairs on the field so no one actually had to walk through cow poop. Fortunately, most of Shasta grew up around animals and the cow pies scattered all around the field wasn't much of a distraction so the focus remained on the graduates. The smell was kept to a minimum in the cool of the morning, but the manure was starting to ripen in the sun by the time we finished. The kids spent most of the ceremony holding theirs noses and making gagging sounds behind me. I didn't turn around, because I didn't blame them. I marked that year off the perfection list before we ever started Pomp and Circumstance. What we had there was a failure to communicate if I could invoke Cool Hand Luke.

Boomer and I had run the teachers through practice the previous afternoon after letting all the students out at noon. It was traditional for us to go through the ceremony and then have the Annual Shasta High Golf Tournament out at the Country Club. The tournament provided an opportunity to relax, unwind a bit after a long school year, and also was an outing for us to see each other in a social setting as opposed to a regular school day. Unfortunately, some of our faculty took the unwinding part a little more seriously than others and a year didn't go by that at least one golf cart or a golfer didn't wind up in a pond.

Brent Jorde, the golf coach, organized the event and the country club was kind enough to hold us a spot each year as an appreciation gift. Since Brent set up the teams and liked his class schedule, I never had to worry since I was always on the team with Brent and Spud Newcomb, the girl's basketball coach. I was their D player and both of them were scratch golfers. Our fourth team member varied every year depending on who got lucky and Brent felt like deserved a shot to ride with the winners. It was nice to be around people that wanted to make sure the boss was happy and I enjoyed being able to go somewhere to have fun and not worry about being responsible for one thing.

The golf was fun in itself since I only played about once a year and this was it. I knew principals that were great golfers. I also knew it took a lot of practice to be great and I figured I could be a great principal or a great golfer, but not both. So far, golf was second. Playing a scramble format, my ball was used maybe once or twice, mostly as a courtesy, but I got to hit every shot and we still won.

The best part was the awards ceremony afterwards out on the patio. A lot of the folks that didn't want to play still showed up for the awards. By awards time the unwinding had been going on for about four hours and many were well on their way to being relaxed. The non-golfers showed up early enough to be in the running for most relaxed so by the time the prizes were given out the atmosphere was festive. I tried to spot my line leaders for graduation to see if they were going to be sober enough by the morning and most seemed to be holding steady. I had fine-tuned my selection process and they had a good time, but felt a responsibility to do well.

Brent had a good sense of humor and plenty of time with his light load of classes along with coaching both girls and boys golf so he had some great awards. He was able to hustle the local businessmen since he was born in Shasta and his daddy owned half of one of the banks. He also knew a couple of gals from over at the Lucky Strike in north Fort Worth that he recruited to help pass out prizes. They usually dressed like the ring girls at a heavyweight-boxing match, which meant they came with professional grade equipment and most of it was visible. The faculty that showed up knew it was all in fun and after the first time, the more prudent ones stayed away. I didn't notice Bitty in the crowd again this year.

With the day headed towards sundown, the burden of the year and a heavy dose of alcohol began to take its toll. Most of the prizes had been awarded, which included a spa day given to one of our grizzled old male math teachers that reminded me of Lurch, to a gift certificate for a box of condoms down at the local pharmacist awarded to one of the sweet middle aged English teachers with a wicked sense of humor. All she had to do was go and pick them up. She cracked up along with everyone else since we all knew she was sweet on the pharmacist. At her age, most suspected that probably should have said lifetime supply.

Depending on Brent's mood, he had a prize for me at the end. Sometimes he felt like poking the bear and sometimes I guess he decided it wasn't worth it. This year must have been a year he figured there had been enough grief and I probably didn't need to be hassled any more. I actually liked the prizes and was never offended, but I also knew that most of these folks weren't comfortable drinking around their boss, much less giving him a feminine product or being awarded a free lesson as the prize for worst golfer.

The best one ever was a motorcycle ride on the back of a Harley. I had always wanted a motorcycle and back when motorcycles began to be mainstream as opposed to just thug and street gang transportation, I had gone and taken the safety course to get my license. I was married then and that particular wife made me a deal that I could have a motorcycle or I could have her. Fortunately, at the time we were somewhat happily married so I opted to keep her. She promptly stuck every newspaper article about motorcycle wrecks on the refrigerator until it was hard to find the handle to get a glass of milk. By the time she found her a new boyfriend and made the choice for me, I was so afraid of dying and her saying 'I told you so' that I never went and bought one.

The faculty at Shasta had picked up on my obsession with Harleys after a couple of years and my talking abut them so one year at the golf awards ceremony, Brent gave me a free ride on a Harley, which so happened to be driven by one of the Lucky Strike girls. I don't know how funny it looked for a man in golfing shorts, wearing a helmet, to be riding down the highway behind a well-developed young lady in a bikini whose long blonde hair was slapping me in the face while I held on for dear life, but it was a time I will always remember. I know I had a tight grip on her waist, but honestly, all I remember is the feel of the machine and the wind rushing past. A taste of freedom.

The night ended without another bike ride for me or anything else, which was fine because everyone was laughing and had a good time. As far as I knew, we had been able to pull Coach Lawson out of the lake on number twelve with only scrapes and bruises and that was the only casualty of the tournament that ended on a high note. I shook hands and wished everyone a safe trip home, thanked Brent for another fine job, and started towards my pickup and home.

II.

I started every graduation day the same. I rose before the sun came up and sat with a cup of coffee out on my balcony. At the end of May in Texas, the mornings were the nicest, coolest times of the whole day and it was important to savor them. I also couldn't sleep, which was the main reason I was up. I had gone over every detail in my head at least twenty times before I dozed off and the few times I fell asleep, I was chasing someone or falling, presumably off the stage. It was better to get up and deal with reality than struggle in my dream world over problems I didn't know I had.

As the sun crept over the horizon, I stood at the balcony railing of my upstairs bedroom like the Pope at St. Peter's Square, and delivered my speech. His crowds probably out numbered mine since I spoke mostly to a couple of jackrabbits, a few gophers, and I'm sure a snake or two. I delivered my speech with gusto since no one was within a mile of where I was standing. Doing it loud and live helped me practice. I repeated it several times using voices of famous stars or singers until I could do it without looking at my notes for more than a reference or a pause. That was important to me.

Once I was satisfied, I went in to shower and put on my one dark suit for the most solemn occasion of the year, in my eyes at least. Dealing with some of the less cultured families, it sometimes sounded like WWF or NASCAR with the cheering and air horns. When the air horns got so bad, we brought in a couple of off duty cops to escort people out and most of that stopped with a few exceptions and they were discreet little toots for a sibling walking across the stage. We all had our beliefs I guess. Success was finding the happy medium of what I could live with and what the masses wanted. It wasn't all about me; I kept trying to tell myself. I didn't always listen.

When I got to the school, Boomer and Mary Nell, my counselor, were working with the students on adjusting their gowns and straightening their caps. As they did, they discreetly checked for any contraband that a student might try to sneak in. Of course, patting them all down was impossible and might have gotten us thrown in jail, but we had been turned down for a screener to run the kids through as giving the public the 'wrong idea' about our students so we fudged it a little at times by 'smoothing out wrinkles in gowns'. A lot of trust had to go into this process and also knowing the kids over the years, it was easy to pick out the most likely pranksters and do some serious smoothing, which they usually needed anyway so it all worked out. Later on, closer to time, Boomer and Mary Nell would line the students up behind their line leaders and give them the coveted card with their name on it, pre-printed to save alterations. Sometimes, as smart as our announcer was, he could get caught up in the routine and simply read cards as he saw them flash before his eyes. Ima Dumass wasn't one of our students and didn't need to be recognized.

Shelley and Donna were putting programs on the stage along with the flowers that had just been delivered. They would finish and stand by the doors passing out programs until the ceremony actually started and anyone coming in after that could 'pickup their own damn program' out of a chair. Donna was pulling double duty as a greeter and a proud mom so she had no intention of missing one second of the ceremony. There was a time none of us expected her Dora to live this long much less graduate. Being our first Goth student with the black clothes and snarly look, we called her Child of Darkness or COD. Turns out she just needed attention and surprisingly was smart as a whip. It was going to be a special day for that family.

I made my way backstage to the director's office where I had a coffeepot set up for the board members and Super Dan. They were supposed to meet me in the back so I could know they were present and then I could get them on stage in an orderly fashion. Their egos were too great to actually sit backstage so most of them roamed around the auditorium, glad handing the parents as if they were running for Governor of Texas, or interfering with Boomer and Mary Nell while they tried to line up the kids. Margaret had the decency to sit back in the office with me and share a cup of coffee for the few minutes I had before I went through my final check of seating, stage, sound, lights, and then brief the students participating in the program. I saved that until right before the show started so they would surely not forget. But they did.

I made my rounds and everything was in its place and the students were all lined up, which meant we were just minutes away from my first perfect graduation. I slipped back stage and put my coat on, gave the board members their final instructions about passing out the diplomas, and reminded Super Dan to shake hands with the kids before they got to the diploma table. Everyone was a veteran of several ceremonies and knew what was supposed to happen, but if this was going to be perfect, I wanted to remind them once again. Their biggest concern was which one of them would give diplomas to certain students. Most chose relatives and kids of friends and then the other students were given diplomas by whoever happened to be standing there. The selection process was critical and sometimes appeared to have the comical seriousness of a fantasy football draft since it was another way to curry favor with the community and have their picture handing a diploma to their child hanging on a family's wall for eternity. It was go time so I lined the 'dignitaries' up and led them onstage.

It was about this time each year that the nervous energy that had been building in me for weeks suddenly turned to a calm serene feeling. Once I was on stage with the spotlights blinding me from seeing much past the first few rows, my mind must have realized that everything else that was fixing to happen was in somebody else's hands and I had no control. I loved that feeling. Of course there was enough concern left to keep me awake and alert.

By the time we suited up our senior members in caps and gowns to walk down the isle, our band would not be large enough to play *Pomp and Circumstance*. We always used a CD, which wasn't a bad idea anyway since it was steady and there was no way it was going to miss a note unless of course it got scratched. I nodded towards the sound booth and was thankful to see my theater arts teacher's face and not Joe Bob's naked butt humping away. The first perfect graduation ceremony was now officially under way. No matter how many times I heard it, *Pomp and Circumstance* always brought a lump to my throat. Okay, just between you and me, I have a sentimental side. Just don't tell anyone.

I could see Boomer and Mary Nell on each side of the aisle giving each student a once over and a nod to go as they kept the spacing consistent and looked for bedazzled mean girls. My top two line-leaders that were chosen for their dependability and had served faithfully for three years now led the march down the center aisle and onto the first row. The next teacher's job was to shove the kid in front of them from the line ahead into the row until the student could sit down on the last remaining seat, before they turned onto their row and the process started again. What had happened in the past were kids spread out as they stood in a general space instead of in front of their seats and it looked like there wasn't enough seats left so the incoming students would start a new row screwing up the alphabet. Teachers in the back pushed the students in no matter what because when everyone actually sat down, surprise, they all had a seat. Except the one year when we miscounted and had one boy running around like musical chairs trying to find a seat when the song ended. But that wasn't happening today. This was perfect graduation day.

Row after row filed in and I smiled at the students who were half asleep, but starting to recognize the moment and the excitement that went along with it. When the last student made it to their row and the last teacher had her place, the music stopped and nobody moved. The rule was you stand until you were told to sit and sit until you were told to stand. We had some opening business before any sitting would be taking place.

114

Like a theatrical director, I eyeballed my invocation student, Marcia Stanwick, class parliamentarian, who refocused in time to start up the stage steps to lead the prayer. The script called for another student to lead the pledges right afterwards so I'm scanning the rows while God was being invoked to bless this special day. Sure enough just before the Amen, Scotty Culpepper bounded on stage as Marcia exited stage right as directed. Smooth as glass!

After the pledges, a recording of the Star Spangled Banner was played, a version I had picked for its direct and no nonsense approach that lasted a minimum amount of time. I didn't need a Whitney Houston five-minute version on graduation day. I then I stepped to the podium and motioned for the students to sit. This was another moment of truth. Did they all have a place? After a little shuffling and reseating it turned out they did indeed have a seat and all the rows were filled. Perfect so far. As a group, we let out a collective breath and relaxed for the first time in about two hours.

I gave my usual welcome, recognizing the parents as the true honorees on this day and thanked families for driving all the way in to help us celebrate. I announced the scholarship winners by having them stand at their seats and this year we had students that were awarded several million dollars in scholarship money thanks to Mary Nell staying after their lazy butts to fill in the paperwork. Their parents should pitch in and buy Mary Nell a car with all the money she was going to save them over the next four years.

As expected, Kelsey and Kneisha were the top grossers. They had led every club and organization at Shasta High as well as participated in volleyball, while also being named All American cheerleaders so it wasn't surprising that they had a lot of different choices. Both had committed to play ball at Midwestern up in Wichita Falls so their families and friends could come watch the games and they could come home on weekends if they wanted. The other monies they had been awarded would help with the difference so they should be able to go to school with out worrying about money. As much help as they had been to me, I felt they deserved every penny they got.

115

They had practically run the school the last two years, keeping the students in line and all going in the right direction. I should probably write them a check myself, but if my calculations were correct, they were now worth more than I was. Maybe they'd hire me when they set out to run the world.

Surprising to everyone but me, Dora, our COD, ran a close third. Her scholarships were all academic awards and she would be attending college pretty much expense free. I watched her mother as I read the list of awards and I had never seen anyone prouder. Dora tried to act bored and nonchalant about the whole thing, but couldn't help but smile when she saw the surprised faces of all those around her. I couldn't even imagine what she would wind up doing, but I hoped I lived long enough to know. I figured it would be amazing.

When I had finished, I introduced our Salutatorian and Valedictorian, which not surprisingly, were Kneisha and Kelsey. Ordinarily, each would give a speech, but they had come to me a few weeks ago and asked to give one together. I had never been asked such a thing before and as scary as the ceremony was as a whole, the scariest moment was when you put a student in front of a microphone without any control as to what was going to come out of their mouths. I had always asked for a copy of speeches ahead of time and offered to help any student practice, even those praying. But I had learned that wasn't a fail-safe method.

A few years ago, a young man was named salutatorian and he handed in his speech right on time and even ran through it for me. The speech was great with the right amount of humor to balance out the seriousness about life and stuff. The day of graduation, he stood up and gave the identical speech, all good things and well wishes, but did so in a combination rap, stand up comedy routine. He went on for what seemed like days and Super Dan was having a coronary as he was tugging at my sleeve to pull the kid's ass off the stage. I knew pulling him off the stage would create an even bigger distraction since the kids were eating it up, clapping and yelling, egging him on. He was the class clown and funny as hell, with a lot of brains to go with it.

The agony finally ended, but the phone calls lasted a few days. Each one had the same basic theme about how insulting it was to invite family in for the ceremony and have them see what was supposed to be one of the smartest kids in Shasta pull such a stunt. If that's the smartest kid, then God help the rest of those poor dumb bastards. I, of course, always asked if they heard the message. Did they hear the good things he was actually saying? Of course they hadn't. All they heard was his presentation and assumed it was something bad. How often does that happen in life? Working with high school kids for this long, I had learned a long time ago that to find the real kid you had to get past the surface because everyone of them, bar none, were Christmas presents.

A few days after graduation, I ran into his mom at Mayfield's grocery when I needed to pick up some razor blades and she thanked me for not interrupting and letting him finish. She had heard the ugliness in town and knew it wasn't popular, but she knew he was a good kid and meant well. I told her no problem, wished them well, paid for the blades, and went on home. I knew it would blow over as all things did. Some people just like to pass judgment and many times it's the ones with the most faults doing the judging.

When Kelsey and Kneisha came to me with their duet speech idea I sat them down and talked to them sternly about how they couldn't mess around or make a mockery of the ceremony. Kneisha rose to her full five foot five and looked me straight in the eye as she leaned over my desk totally insulted.

"Mr. Masters," she said in her always at high volume voice. "Who do you think you are talking to? We aren't some ragged assed scoundrels that all of sudden showed up in your office wanting to talk at graduation! You know us! We been running this school for the last two years and we made dang sure our clubs and the kids did right. We are proud of Shasta High and the last thing we would want to do is embarrass ourselves or this school!" She was breathing hard, nostrils flaring, and her eyes were wide enough to see mostly white heat coming my way. I was deservedly put in my place.

"Kneisha, you are absolutely right. I owe you and Kelsey an apology," I said very remorseful. "I have given you the keys to this school and pretty much let you have the run of the campus night and day. Why would I think I couldn't trust you now?"

"Dang right!" was all she said as she plopped back in her chair and continued to burn me with the evil eye.

"You two work out what you want to say and how you want to say it. If you want to run it by me fine and if you don't...I'll trust you to do the right thing," I said less convinced than I let on. The most trustworthy eighteen year-old on Earth is still eighteen years old and three years away from a fully developed common sense. I was going to have to give myself more than one talking to over the next few weeks, but I had to put my faith in these girls.

So here they came to the stage all smiles. I had neither seen nor asked what they intended to say and now the pain in my stomach reached an all time high. Its hard to have faith period, its harder to have faith in kids, but some you just have to trust. My perfect graduation was now in the hands of two of the best students I had ever had.

As I should have expected, over the next ten minutes the girls spoke with eloquence and humor, recognizing friends and family. They honored teachers present and from the past that had been instrumental in their lives. They spoke of dreams and goals and in the end gave me a nod of thanks for allowing them the freedom to grow and become adults. I felt honored and ashamed at the same time for doubting them or putting them in the same category with the typical knot headed kids. I led the standing ovation as they finished. I didn't expect to have any one like them come along again. I think those girls were one of those once in a lifetime kind of things that I didn't appreciate enough until they were gone.

III.

As the ceremony continued with a musical number by a quartet of senior choir students, I started feeling like this might be the one, the graduation where everything was going to fall into place. The scariest parts of course would be when Super Dan spoke and right at the very end. One never knew.

We had tried cordless microphones a few years ago to give us a little more flexibility and movement about the stage. It seemed like a good idea especially when I thought I might be able to walk back and forth like a TV evangelist regaling the students with my wit and humor. I had hooked up Super Dan with his mike, showing him the mute switch to push when he got ready to talk and warned him not to touch anything until it was time for his speech. Just as I was giving the last minute instructions to the board members and we were getting ready to go out on stage in front of a packed auditorium, I heard a noise like a squeaking door and then a zipper. This was followed a few seconds later by the sound of someone urinating and was accompanied by a blast of gas. This, of course, was being broadcast across the entire auditorium and people were starting to look at each other especially when the whistling began and the water continued to flow with a stop/start rhythm for what seemed like eternity punctuated by two smaller explosions of gas. I supposed I had that to look forward to as I aged, but hopefully it wouldn't be broadcast for public consumption. I made a very quick trip to the back of the auditorium and shut the sound system down as opposed to try and find Super Dan. Fortunately, with the power cut, the sounds ended, but not before we were treated to one more gaseous blast and a loud sigh.

Needless to say we abandoned the cordless mike idea and I used a brief welcome prior to the students coming in to apologize for the technical difficulties of our having picked up some sort of television broadcast out of Oklahoma City. Some bought the story, others had their doubts, but nobody could argue and we all hoped to forget what we had heard as soon as possible. Super Dan had come strolling back in to the director's room checking his zipper with a satisfied smile on his face, good to go for at least another hour, hopefully. I said nothing, but took his apparatus explaining it was faulty. As the musical number came to a close, I shuttered thinking about the cordless mike fiasco, but had often wondered how they would have worked. I still wanted to move when I talked. Maybe someday I will have the courage to try again. Maybe using an eight second delay. Maybe.

My speech was something I took a lot of pride in. I tried to personalize it for each class and combine a little humor with a serious thought or two. I had really stressed over giving one the first time or two until I realized that most students never heard what I said, the ones that did forgot by the time they had walked out the door so the most important thing was not to say something stupid that a parent might remember for years. They were the ones that actually listened. I took it as a challenge each year to find one key word that might stick in the students' brains and be helpful to them down the road. I had no way of knowing if that had happened or not, but it's what motivated me to prepare and practice. I gave my speech, looked each student in the face, and knew it was time to wrap up when I saw eyes roaming and a yawn or two. That usually started around the five to seven minute mark if I was doing really well. I wished them well, I asked God to bless them even though that was violating their Constitutional right of separating church and state. So far no one had threatened to sue me and hopefully God had indeed blessed the kids. I certified to Super Dan and the board that all the sleepy eyed students sitting in front of them had actually passed all their requirements and should be given a diploma regardless of how surprising it might be and then I introduced Super Dan.

I sat down and started mouthing a silent prayer that I didn't have to tackle him and pretend I accidently fell, or pull him down from behind and tell everyone he had a stroke. I had considered all these things and more in previous years, but never had to employee such drastic tactics. He had managed to insult more than a few people by some of the things he had said, but when the parents complained to me, I tell them I'm not his boss and although I agreed with everything they said, they need to tell it to the board.

Super Dan's graduation speech was just like his address to the faculty or what I imagined he would give even if he were invited to speak to a joint session of Congress or the U. N. His ego convinced him that his spontaneous wit and charm were enough and simply sharing his thoughts of the moment should make us all feel blessed and grateful. When he started off 'On the way over here I was thinking…' gave me a pretty good idea of the preparation that went into the message he was fixing to share with us.

This morning he got to telling stories and the next thing we knew he was back in Head Football coach's mode and talking to the students as if they were fixing to take the field for the state championship game he coached thirty years ago. Sis Boom Bah. He was rolling, that's for sure, and then right at the end he channeled General Patton to summarize his thought for the kids. He challenged them to rush out the door this very minute, grab the world by the throat, and kick it in the ass before it knew what hit it. I held my breath hoping they wouldn't leave quite yet since none of them had been given their diploma and fortunately they either realized that as well or had tuned Super Dan out sometime earlier. None left as Super Dan sat down with a satisfied smirk on his face as if he just delivered the Gettysburg address. I actually wished he had and been through about fifteen minutes earlier.

I took inventory and realized as unconventional as that speech might have been, I felt like we were still unscathed. He hadn't incited a riot or insulted any particular race or gender so I felt like we were still on pace to perfection. I categorized Super Dan as an act of God, something I couldn't control and therefore no harm no foul. We moved on to the name-calling and diploma awarding as the line leaders began the process of bringing kids to the stage.

Our announcer read the name off the card he was handed as the student walked across the stage while they shook my hand, Super Dan's hand, and then a board member's hand that in turn handed them their diploma cover. Shake with the right and reach with the left. The process was repeated over and over again until all students had been recognized. It was at this point that students had a little fun handing me nickels or quarters. Some years it was marbles. The worst class brought golf balls, which would have been nice had they been Titleist, but being the buttholes they were, they raided the driving range and picked up the scraggliest red striped balls they could find.

The point of the ritual I guess was to see how I managed under pressure once the number of items began to stack up. I used my coat pockets to handle most items and I like the coin thing the best since in the past I had gathered enough to pay for a hamburger and fries afterwards. The golf balls? Well that was a mess until one of the coaches saw my plight and stood off stage as I chunked them one after another to him and he sacked them up and returned them to the driving range. Being hidden behind the podium from most of the audience helped, but the ones that saw me probably wondered what the heck was going on. Fortunately, in the aftermath and celebration the golf balls were forgotten.

As Erin Zweicher's name was called, I realized we had managed to stay in alphabetical order through the whole program. As she made her way across the stage, got her photo snapped with a smiling board member, and then headed back to her seat, I paused long enough to take a deep breath before I introduced the graduating class one last time and moved into Def Con three, the time when the kids are standing, the alma mater would begin to play and opportunity for chaos to break out was at it's highest. I was so close to perfection that I could taste it and wished little Erin would hustle her self back to her seat before there was too much dead time. Students can't handle dead time and felt the need to create activity to fill the void. I wanted to be the only one filling voids.

As she turned down her row I motioned for the kids to stand, presented them to the audience who applauded loud and long, while I motioned for the sound booth to cue up the alma mater. This brought everyone back to order and we all raised our hands to form a Coyote paw and mouthed the words about how we love the Green and White, Coyotes fight, fight, fight.

When practicing the teachers the day before, I spent more time with what happened at this point of the program than anything else. I explained the kids would be brain dead and totally disoriented without a clue what to do next other than to throw their hats, hoot, holler, or in someway express themselves, which can be in many unacceptable ways. The line leaders job was to grab the first kid on the front rows and shove them up the

122

exit aisle to get movement and continue to grab kids until everyone realizes they need to be walking after their friends out the door. My goal was to get them out of the auditorium and then the rest of their life was their own and my day of celebration could begin. I was within seconds of perfection and I could feel the anticipation building within myself as the last note sounded and I saw my two line leaders reach for their kid and to begin shoving.

It was at this point that time stood still and my world shifted to slow motion. In the instant between the last note of the alma mater and when the audience began to cheer, almost to a kid, a can was slipped from under their gowns and instead of caps being thrown to the ceiling, a canopy of pink silly string arced overhead covering all the students and teachers under its web. I saw the cans coming out as a person might see a weapon being drawn during a hold up on TV. It was achingly slow, but I knew I was helpless since my body would be moving in slow motion as well and they had us outnumbered ten to one. I saw line leader faces turn to shock with eyes bulging, mouths grimaced, as they reached for the nearest can, but it was too late. The coordinated effort was a work of skill and practice or at least dumb luck, because we were defenseless to stop the carnage.

I heard Super Dan say, "What the hell...?" and some of the board members laughed thinking it was part of the celebration and a jolly good time it was. I simply chose to remain stoic and unmoving, refusing to give the kids the satisfaction of seeing me cringe. As I waited for the destruction to end, I mentally marked this year off as a candidate for perfection. Close only counted in horseshoes, hand grenades, and strip joints. I watched as the teachers finally got some traction and began moving the kids out of the auditorium and then looked back at me to see what they should do. I just shook my head and said don't worry about it. Just make sure they keeping moving right on out the door and into the real world. From here on out it was between them, the police, and God. I wished them well.

I walked off the stage and was looking for Raymond Terrell my custodian who I knew was back stage waiting to do one final cleaning before his weekend began. He, of course, was getting some overtime and didn't mind a Saturday out of the house, especially his house. I was about to give him some really good news. He was fixing to be working longer than had been expected, which meant more money and more time away from his nutcase family. The thing about silly string was that it turned to powder as opposed to being sticky. Raymond would be vacuuming most of the front half of the auditorium this afternoon, which is why he smiled when I told him. At least someone was happy.

I started towards the door to make my way through the auditorium, down the hall to my office to close up my business for the day, while the families snapped pictures and graduates took one last photo of themselves and their friends. They would eventually leave to eat out together or go back home for a family cookout. Bottom line was they were celebrating and what had happened five minutes ago was long forgotten... except by me. I needed to quit taking this kind of stuff so personally. I knew the kid's antics weren't directed at me and this class didn't have a mean bone in its body. They were just having fun and had no idea how much it bothered me. I realized it was me that was going to have to change. I couldn't remember these kids for this minute of madness and forget the great four years we had together. I was giving myself a pep talk as I re-entered the auditorium by the stage headed towards the hall in the back when I saw Dora Simmons coming towards me.

"Hey, I was looking for you," she said pretty straight forward. Dora was never much with words and when she was at her Goth peak, even getting a grunt out of her was hard. She had made a lot of progress and knowing she was going to college made me smile.

"Hey Dora, just trying to find the custodian to start sweeping up y'alls celebration." I said with a little harder edge than I meant to.

"Cool, huh?" she snorted with a half smile. "I didn't think we could do it"

I could tell she and the others saw the coordinated effort a masterpiece and a gigantic success. I chose not to try and explain. I knew then I didn't have to worry about anyone remembering my speech or Super Dan's for that matter, which was an added bonus. I assumed the kids had been so focused on their go signal; they probably missed the whole ceremony.

"You promised me a hug," Dora said coming out of her reverie. "I want it."

Now it was my turn to smile. When I had my come to Jesus meeting with Dora during her sophomore year, trying to reach her and find a way for her to be somebody, I had promised to tell everyone she really wasn't the bad ass she portrayed herself to be unless she focused on her grades and graduated. When all the sputtering and fuming had finally gotten out of the way she realized I was on her side. We became friends and I promised her a hug at graduation if she made it. At the time, she scoffed like that would be the last thing she wanted from me, but I guessed she didn't forget.

Feeling once again like an ass for getting so wound up over some stupid silly string that would vacuum up and realizing what I was actually missing, I wrapped my arms around Dora and told her how proud of her I was. I made sure she knew she could always count on me.

"Thank you," she said in a muffled voice with her face pressed against my chest.

"Dora this is all you. You made this happen. I was just glad to be part of it," I said reassuringly.

"No. Not me. Thanks for my mom," she said a little more firm.

"You're mom?" I asked

"Thanks for getting her a job. She's a good person and has tried really hard for us. She needed something good to happen for her and you helped." She said this time looking me in the eye.

I had know idea the layers and depth that made up this child, but I knew there was a lot more to her than anyone could possibly realize. "I just figured if she was here in the office, I'd get to see you when you came home to visit." I replied trying to lighten the mood since neither one of us really wanted to do any crying.

"Yea, right. You just think she's hot and want to date her. Just think you could be my daddy!" she laughed and we walked up the aisle towards the back with my arm around her shoulder.

IV.

When everyone had finally made their way to the parking lot and I heard Raymond vacuuming away, whistling like a man out on parole, I slid my jacket off and loosened my tie on the way to my truck. Let the count down begin. The next twenty-four hours were mine and I intended to enjoy them. I had a whole lot of adrenaline still flowing so I cranked up the volume on my ZZ Top CD and sang along. The pick up knew the way and I was in peak form all the way home. From this high, I would gradually begin to drain away the adrenaline, the cares and worries would seep away with it, and as if I were using a slow motion anesthesia, I would eventually fall sound asleep sometime late tonight and sleep the sleep of the righteous. But that's later. Now it's My Time.

I threw my suit in a pile on the floor and made a mental note to take it to the cleaners so it would be ready for the next solemn event, hopefully not before next May. I slipped on my favorite pair of shorts, a t-shirt, and my sandals. I grabbed a cooler of beer as I went out the back door and opened up the grill to load it up with charcoal. I covered it with lighter fluid and then put the flame to it. With a burst of heat, the party started. I sat in my lawn chair drinking beer, waiting for the fire to reach perfection, knowing I had steaks ready to cook, along with a couple of sausages, and some corn on the cob. That was my traditional after graduation meal. I sometimes cooked late into the night, rummaging around my freezer for any meat I may have overlooked and then having leftovers for a couple of weeks. My Time meant I did what I felt like and right now I felt like watching the fire blaze and the drinking beer under my carport.

I was on my third cold one and the charcoal was starting to turn white around the edges when I heard a car turn into my driveway. I heard the gravel crunch under the wheels as it slowly rounded the corner and pulled towards the back. I smiled as the front of Ms. Shelly's Buick came into view and she stopped in her usual spot. Her chair was already set up and I had a blender full of her favorite concoction already made up.

She wasn't much of a drinker, but she knew a special occasion when she saw one. In the name of celebration, she had been known to have a margarita or two and the times I gave her enchiladas along with those margaritas, I sometimes got lucky. Ms. Shelly would be staying long into the evening as we let the school year roll off our shoulders as we watched the sunset from the balcony. If I didn't start slurring my words too early, we might even have a little under the sheets celebration. I suspected she had a lot of stress needing to be released just like I did and I was pretty good at helping her get rid of her tension.

For now, I sat looking at her with a frosty glass in her hand, her khaki shorts showing off her legs, and wearing a pink Rangers cap with her haired pulled through the hole in the back. I savored every minute of My Time because I knew it was fleeting and wouldn't come around again for another year. Sharing it with Shelly made it even sweeter.

Keeping Austin Weird

1.

Shelly had stayed late into the night as we let the aches and pains of the year slide off our backs while laughing about some of the things that were whole lot funnier now than when they actually happened. We talked about kids, the good ones, the bad ones, or at least the ones that felt the need to act bad a lot of the times. Shelly got down in the floor laughing about my visit last fall with Raymond Terrell and his family with so many kids they were overlapping themselves at school. How confused I had looked coming our of the office and how proud he looked having been placed in charge of the whole situation being a school employee and all. Since it was his two daughters and a granddaughter, of course he should have been in charge to begin with.

We relived the infamous Jell-O wrestling with Boomer and the fact he still had no idea his body had been taken over by aliens when he almost killed me in front of the whole school. Shelly laughed harder at that story than I did since I'd had several nightmares about suffocating since then only to wake up and find my pillow over my face. One thing about it, the kids loved it and talked about it the rest of the year. We made the centerfold of the yearbook. I was immortalized being held aloft by Boomer the Giant. The fear on my face was evident.

By the time we got to the cheerleaders' car wash we both'd had plenty to drink and neither one of us could tell it without cracking up. Like a good fishing story, every time you told it, it got better and the fish got bigger. By now the girls were dancing on the car hoods and most of the men of Shasta were lined up with video cameras making home movies, while Robin's mom was serving cocktails wearing her gold slinky bikini with her professional grade goods on display. I think we laughed harder in order to forget that the following Monday I had come within minutes of losing my job and maybe even my career.

By the time the sun started to set, we had laughed ourselves out and my adrenaline rush was rapidly depleting. We spent some time in the porch swing on my balcony and then a few more minutes in my bedroom. I wouldn't be seeing Shelly for a week and I needed to be close to her for as long as possible.

Holding her and smelling her perfume balanced out the rest of my life no matter how crazy it got. I was leaving for Austin this morning and Shelly would be in church. She had left me smiling and a man with no cares as she drove down the drive way and home to study her Sunday school lesson shortly after nine.

II.

The first week in June was always reserved for our principal's convention and the date was no coincidence. Our organization put together a really nice three-day event with all kinds of meetings and presentations for those that wanted to attend. It was all window dressing for the actual purpose of the week, which was to let loose and unwind with a few thousand other junior high and high school principals that had survived another school year. Austin had experience with conventioneers and with the University of Texas located close to downtown; Austin's finest had plenty of practice dealing with drunken juvenile behavior. The differences between the UT kids and us were we had some sense, spent our own money, and had careers to think about. Other than that, Sixth Street was overtaken for a week by a bunch of over grown kids that tried their best to drink their way to happiness and stay up at least until midnight.

As I drove down I-35 on a beautiful June morning, I had an old Beach Boys CD playing, which was also a tradition. There was just something about the Beach Boys that made the trip feel like a vacation. With it being June and school being out, well...this was as close to Endless Summer that I would get. I did a mental run through of my schedule for the week to make sure I had an even balance of networking and relaxing. Networking meant going to the Convention Center and saying hello to all my friends I had made over the years. With as many moves as I had made, I knew people from a number of different districts across Texas and I had also trained a few assistants that had their own schools now. It was good to see them all and find out how they made the year. Telling war stories just came naturally when the booze stated flowing.

If I knew someone presenting on a topic that interested me, I might stick my head in a room and listen if I could sit in the back. I rarely wanted to stay for the whole hour or hour and a half. I figured I could get most of the information off their handout and honestly, I wasn't here to learn this week. I would start thinking about next year when I go back and if I needed something, I would find it then. When I was younger, I spent more time at the Convention Center and less time on Sixth Street. I had learned better over the years. The need to relax was important so a person didn't get wound up too tight. If the pressure wasn't released at the end of each year it built up and added on to the next. That's was a sure fire recipe for burnout or a breakdown. Release the pressure. It was a medically sound reason for partying. Four out of five doctors recommended it. The fact they were Ed.D's instead of medical doctors shouldn't make a difference. Right?

Some of the major suppliers of school stuff like class rings or yearbooks would throw a party for all the principals that used their services. It was a thank you of sorts or I guess bribery...kickbacks? We didn't care since it was all you could eat and all you could drink, which meant that they shelled out a hundred or two hundred dollars per head, but I figured they still made a lot of money or they wouldn't keep doing it every year.

My friends and I would do some serious networking at these events. This is where the real stories got told and the party served as a warm up for Sixth Street that would start hopping about eight each night. Principal's started earlier than college kids did, but then we got through earlier as well. The free drinks also made the night cheaper since most of us had pretty well reached our limit on the free booze supplied by the distributors and only had to buy a drink to get in the door on Sixth Street before needing to start back to the hotel.

The real surprise was that so few people actually lost their jobs as a result of the events of the week. There was ample opportunity and it was usually the younger ones that came close. Fortunately Austin's finest had a sense of humor or at least had been given good training concerning the educators that took care of their kids during the school year. About the only way someone wound up with a mug shot was if they tried to drive, if they got scared and tried to run, or, and this was mostly the younger principals, they figured they would just whip the cops ass right there on the street and walk away. That was never a good choice. Old dudes managed to get hauled in occasionally for propositioning a girl on the corner that turned out to be part of a sting operation and it was all caught on videotape. I'm sure if you could see the tapes, the girl would be trying to dissuade the crazy old fool, but to no avail.

Most of the time a cop would take out your wallet, give a cabbie a twenty, and pour you into the backseat to be delivered back to your hotel. They had all the publicity they needed when arresting pro football players that came back in the summer and felt bullet proof. Once the all brawn and no brain millionaires started tearing up a bar, the cops had no choice so they always got a mug shot. I smiled to myself in anticipation of the coming few days. I vowed to still have a job on Friday and make Ms. Shelly proud of me.

The first decision a principal had to make was a hotel. It had to be within walking distance to the Convention Center, which most were. It had to be within walking distance of Sixth Street, which most were. It had to have a free breakfast other than cereal in a box and an apple, which eliminated several. And finally, it had to have a happy hour, which narrowed it down to a select few. I had made my choice several years ago and had stayed at the Hamptons each year since. I loved the free breakfast, which was the real stuff meaning I could count on sausage and biscuits with gravy at least three times during the week. And every day at five it was wine and beer along with some nuts and popcorn. A person had to have their priorities. Once that was settled the rest was easy.

III.

I usually arrived Sunday afternoon and met a few friends for happy hour to kick off the week. There were no serious plans for the first night except to go to Chuy's and have Quesadillas with creamy jalapeño sauce. If you were starting to get the idea that there was a lot of tradition involved to the point of being a ritual, then you have been paying attention. I would say it was just me being quirky, but I know everyone else had that same starved for excitement and fun look in their eyes and they knew they only have a limited time to feed their wild side before returning to respectability. After supper, I made my way back to my room since I knew that every bit of my adrenaline and the free fall of My Time would come crashing down tonight. I have to put myself to bed early and let my body regroup to have the stamina to make it through this week. It didn't surprise nor bother me that by eight-thirty I was toast and I rolled over with the television and lamp still on and slept for nine hours.

When I woke up to the sound of the early morning weather report calling for partly cloudy skies and a possibility of afternoon showers, I smiled to myself. The healing had taken place and I was ready for the week. I decided that I was hungry and figured I could beat most of the folks down to the breakfast buffet to get myself some biscuits and gravy. Those that came in on Sunday are here for the legal conference, which made up the program for the first day. About half the principals opted out and since this was a non legislative year there wouldn't be any new laws we needed to know about so most of the program would be beating us over the head with special education laws. Anyone showing up on Sunday like me came for the healing or had their first round of partying last night. Either way I figured to be first in line.

Knowing that it would be principals making up most of the downtown traffic this week, and we treat each other like family, I decided to slip on my sandals and a t-shirt to go with my raggedy shorts I traveled in. Shaving, hair brushing, and teeth bushing would all take place after breakfast. I looked myself in the mirror and decided it would be best not to step outside the hotel since the morning bum patrol might load me up and take me to the nearest soup kitchen. I scoffed as if I actually thought anyone cared or would give me a second look at five-thirty on a Monday morning.

I shuffled down to the elevator and pressed the down button and used spit to mat down part of my hair that was sticking up in the back from laying wrong on the pillow. I used my reflection in a large metal flowerpot to help guide my efforts. I stop when I heard the ding-ding announce the car's arrival and turned to wait for the door to open. As soon as the doors swung open, I stepped in reflexively, looking down, still focused with my hand on the unruly part of my hair. As I looked up, I saw two of the most beautiful stewardesses that I had ever seen. They were immaculate in their navy blue outfits, which included a starched blue shirt with a multi colored scarf, stockings, and heels. Both have their little pull suitcase tucked behind their very tucked behinds and their make-up, being fresh, sparkled in the light and was highlighted by bright red lipstick.

My first thought was 'Well, Hello Ladies!' I'm sure my eyes looked as if someone had set a T-bone steak in front of me. I was just about to speak when my upper brain caught up with my lower brain and said in a very loud voice 'Looked in the mirror lately?' I took quick inventory to see what the damage was and even using the male guide for acceptable appearance, which is much less stringent than the ladies guide for men's respectable appearance, I wasn't able to convince myself I had a shot. This was confirmed by the 'you gotta be kidding me' look that the blonde gave my initial eye popping overture followed by a 'seriously?' from the brunette. I simply turned back towards the front to punch the button for the ground floor when I realized someone had punched every button on the panel. I gave a quick questioning look over my shoulder and the brunette actually spoke and said, "Bummer, huh?"

I wasn't sure if she was referring to the fact there was a joker up at five thirty in the morning pushing all the buttons or that I was stuck in the elevator with two gorgeous women for the next couple minutes while the car stopped on each floor and I looked like dog poop. I simply murmured "um huh", faced the front where I could at least enjoy the smell of their perfume, counted the seconds in the silence, and vowed never ever to leave my room again unless I was ready for action. Dang you Karma. Dang you Big Bu.

Mercifully, the elevator finally came to rest on the ground floor and I stepped out to hold the doors for the ladies to pull their little cases out behind them. I hoped being a gentleman would count for something. I couldn't read the message in the smirk they each gave me as the moved by and on out the front door to the taxi stand, but it probably was some superior feeling of having shot down a guy using only their eyebrows. I reminded myself I had a woman back home that loved me unshaven and with a cowlick and walked confidently to the buffet line happy that I was indeed the first to ladle gravy on piping hot biscuits. What stewardesses?

I finished my breakfast, made my way to my room to freshen up and be better prepared for the return trip back down and then walked over to the Convention Center for some networking. As expected the only people in the elevator this time were two very hung over guys I suspected to be principals, heading to breakfast in last night's clothes. I gave them a superior look since I had already eaten and was dressed for the day. Hah. Amateurs.

The rest of the day was spent mainly outside the presentations talking to different friends who came by and occasionally peeking in to hear snippets of the topic. As expected it was special education documentation and I chose to not hear any more on that subject. We did our best and hopefully I'll be gone before anyone decides we prevented their child from getting an appropriate education especially if they believed it should have included being spoon fed a lesson by a one on one teacher because somewhere in elementary school it was easier to say they were disabled as opposed to spend the extra time needed then to catch them up with the rest of their class. Unfortunately, the kiddo had been paying the price and getting further behind ever since, but don't get me started on that.

Being at the end of the education ladder, high school didn't have the option of passing kids along. We were responsible to fix all the damage done the previous nine years, in four years so students could graduate. Four years if we were lucky. Sometimes we had juniors and seniors move in and then it was next to impossible to make it work.... but we did our best. It always made me angry that many times it wasn't the kids fault, but they were the ones that wound up paying the price. I decided I was getting too worked up for a week in June and started back towards happy hour and the annual Full Moon Howling.

IV.

Very few people in Shasta knew this except Ms. Shelly, but I was a closet musician. My mama started me taking piano lessons when I was five and managed to keep me interested until I entered junior high when I started playing football and learned about girls. I had developed some basic skills, thanks to a couple of very patient ladies that drilled me each week and knew I was lying when I said I practiced, but I hadn't. When I went off to college there was piano in the lobby of the dorm and I found that if you sat down and could play a bluesy number or maybe one of the new rock and roll hits, that girls tended to migrate your direction and hang around as long as you could perform. I guess it was like most things in life or a preview to marriage. Performance is key. I spent many a dateless Friday night with a handful of girls that talked to me all night like I was Elton John requesting one song after another. I of course preferred to be thought of more as Mickey Gilley or at least Billy Joel, but Elton did play a mean piano as long as the girls didn't associate his piano playing with his sexual persuasion and conclude they were related.

I found I spent more time practicing piano in college than I did going to class. I could have majored in Music and come out with better grades. As it was, I managed to scrape by in my education classes and get a diploma, but I had a hobby for life. It turned out that many times I sought out a piano when things were really tough and after a half hour or so of playing, I started feeling better. Since a school always had a piano in the choir room, I knew that at the end of the day or sometimes during class, I could bang out a song or two and feel better.

A few years back, I had gone into a bar on Sixth Street called Beethoven's Fifth, which had just reinvented itself from a grunge bar and before that disco. They had installed a piano in hopes of cashing in on the popularity of the dueling pianos up the street or the one on the corner that everyone seemed to enjoy singing along with while being insulted by the performers.

My friend and I were having a drink and noticed that no one was playing so we asked the waitress. She told us Mondays were really slow and they didn't have anyone come in and play since they lost money. I asked if the manager minded if I played a few numbers, feeling bullet proof since we were on our third bar after happy hour. The manager came out and ask if I could I really play or was I 'just gonna screw around on his equipment'. I assured him I was a trained musician, had played in college (I just told you I had) and respected the instrument that sat across the room. He snorted and said I could have two numbers and if I sucked he would throw me out himself.

I surveyed the room and didn't get much of a feel for what the audience might enjoy since the audience consisted of a couple in the back, an old man in the corner, and my friend. I decided something upbeat might attract attention from the street and bring in a customer or two so I opened with *Crocodile Rock*. It was one of those songs that made you feel good even if you have never heard it before and if you have, you can sing along even if you don't know the words. I was half way through the chorus when I heard the old guy in the back singing harmony with me and the couple had turned to listen and was patting their thighs. I ran through the chorus an extra time since it appeared everyone (all five) was having a good time. When I finished, I received a round of applause from the crowd, which now included the bartender and the waitress.

I took an exaggerated bow and sat down to play another favorite of mine since this was Austin and Robert Earl Keen was a household name. It was June, but when you played *Merry Christmas From the Family* nobody cared what month it was. It didn't take half a song this time before the old feller picked up his mug of beer and moved to a front table so he could join in better and make sure I heard him. A couple from the street walked in clapping and started singing before they sat down. By the time we have gone through the chorus a half dozen times, the house had grown to a dozen. I ended with a flourish and thanked them for their support and started back to my seat. The old feller asked me where I was going and if the show was over. I said I was just given two songs and that was all. He said 'hell no!' and went over to the bar and wanted to know 'what kind of shithole was this place and why couldn't his friend play more'n two songs?' The manger motioned me with his head to get my ass back on stage and I played the rest of the evening. More than once my new friend actually came up and sat on the piano bench with me before the bartender escorted him back to his seat. The second time, I told the big dude to leave him, that he was fine. He did have a pretty good voice and looked a lot like Charlie Daniels. I figured I owed this gig to him so it was partly his show and knowing Austin, it might very well have been Charlie.

My friend had disappeared long before midnight when I finished up hoarse and drunk since the bartender kept sending drinks if I would keep playing. I thanked the crowd of over thirty for their generous applause and was asked by a couple where I would be playing next. As I gathered my thoughts and finished my last drink, the manager came over and asked if I was interested in a permanent job. When I explained I had a permanent job, he offered weekends. What we finally worked out with him was a two-hour slot on the first Monday night of June each year and I promised I would fill his bar. Thus the Annual Full Moon Howlin' was born.

The first year, I simply emailed a few of my friends and asked them to drop by and it has grown into sort of a cult following. Tonight would be our tenth Howlin' and we had starting printing T-shirts that were becoming collector's items among my educator friends. Those that had all of them were considered hardcore howlers. Thinking back to that first night and my lookalike friend Charlie Daniels that pretty much threatened to tear up the place if we didn't get to sing some more, made me smile as I walked towards Sixth Street just as the sun began to go down.

I greeted Maybelle with a hug as I pushed through the door. She was the third manager the club had since I had been playing and each one had been fine with me continuing with basically what had become a principal party. Monday nights were slow as a rule since most street crawlers spent their money and enthusiasm Friday to Sunday. Mondays in the summer were even slower with most of the college kids gone home. Having a night when a house full of fairly sane educators that were awful thirsty for a drink and fun was a boon for the club. We caused very little trouble, we were notoriously generous tippers, especially if we think the waitress might flirt with us, and we hadn't had a good drinking binge in almost a year. What's not to like.

As I took the stage about 9:30 to get everyone warmed up, I saw the usual crowd minus some that had retired, even though I had a couple of friends that drove down just for the Howlin'. I also saw a few new, younger faces, which was encouraging since we needed to keep hope alive among the younger set that would have to carry on our traditions in the future after we were gone and institutions like the Howlin' were now part of educational culture. Where else could you find so many people that couldn't sing a note, have so much fun singing songs from Willie Nelson to Frank Sinatra. Yeah, at least once an evening we sang with enthusiasm how we took the licking and kept on ticking and did it our way.

What you need to understand was my role was like the music minister at the Baptist church on a Sunday morning. I picked out the songs, with a few requests thrown in, got the song started for everyone to jump in and we all sang along as best we could. I put forth a little more effort on the second and third verses, which is where a lot of the crowd got lost having never really sang more than the opening few lines kind of like the third verse of Amazing Grace. Then we all finished with a strong chorus and unlike church we chugged another drink and got ready for the next song.

Since this whole crazy night started with Crocodile Rock, I always opened with it as a traditional way to kick off the party, at least the singing part. Some of the folks had been here since happy hour started at four and they usually sang the loudest up until about eleven when they passed out or their friends poured them into a cab. They were usually either new principals having lived through the first terrifying year, or a veteran that had a major crisis and barely escaped having to work as a greeter for Wal-Mart. We bounced back and forth from country to rock, keeping everyone happy and all the Howlers know that at about eleven we did our Robert Earl Keen trilogy starting with *Gringo Honeymoon*, ripping right into *Merry Christmas From the Family*, and finished with a thunderous *The Road Goes on Forever and the Party Never Ends*.

It was usually after these fifteen minutes of rousing singing that I had to take a break and unload some of the beer I had been drinking to keep my throat moist. I also usually shifted over to some sort of whiskey for the final push. Everyone refilled their glasses or their hands and we took off again singing loud enough that people walking up an down the street peeked their head in and a few took the chance of pushing through the crowd to get a drink and join us. The one thing that Maybelle knew was the cash register never stopped ringing and the bartenders were in constant motion. It was a good night for Maybelle and the girls that were smart enough to volunteer to work a Monday night shift since they usually went home with a lot of bills stuck inside their bra straps and most of them weren't singles.

I mixed in some of the oldie goldie songs with some of the newer ones coming out, trying to keep us current, and the younger folks interested. Usually, there was a new hit that came out that everyone had heard and liked. The great thing about our night was that knowing the words was optional. All we needed was the tune and we took it and ran. We could sing the same song ten times during the night and rarely sing the same words twice. Our unofficial motto that I led off with, and reminded them of several times over the course of the evening was 'the drunker you are, the better I sound'. Each time the whole bar shouted it with me. Truth is a great motivator.

We had a number of women that made up the audience and Elvis was always popular with them. I tried to do my version of the King as I went around the edge of the stage singing a cappella and let them kiss my hands in mock fashion as we all sang *Love me Tender.* I slid right into *Are You Lonesome Tonight* as I invited a lady I had selected to come up on the stage to sit on the piano bench. There were certain qualifications and all of them had to do with looks. I tried to find a newbie who didn't know the routine if I could. When the song ended I interviewed them for the audience finding out their name, where they were from, the usual stuff, and then right on cue we jumped on *A Little Less Conversation a lot More Action Please.*

Fortunately the one's I chose all had a good sense of humor and I usually wound up with at least a kiss on the cheek as they headed back down to their table. I had one especially friendly lady one year that practically jumped on me and we went over backwards off the piano bench to the roaring delight of the crowd. Fortunately, no one was injured, especially me. I found out later that the roar wasn't so much for how affectionate the woman was, but as we went over, she mooned the whole crowd much to their delight.

If *Crocodile Rock* was the official opening number, then Mickey Gilley's *The Girls Always Get Prettier at Closing Time* was the final song of the evening. Just about midnight I usually played the introductory chords and many of the patrons sober enough would moan knowing another Howlin' was coming to a close. We had thought about going longer, but were afraid we would have too many drunken principals staggering down the street, plus closing early on Monday was good for morale especially for the workers with wads of cash in their pocket. Midnight was a good stopping point for me since I rarely sang longer than a half hour at home and never to the level of volume as I did here. Throw in some cigarette smoke and a lot of booze, fun was fun and then it had to end. We all joined in for one last rousing chorus having given the ladies the right to substitute 'the guys always get hornier at closing time' and finished with a laugh and cheer all around. The Tenth Full Moon Howlin' was another success. The folks came, had a good time and had the t-shirt to prove it.

I made my way to a table in the back to talk to a couple of friends I had known a long time and who had made the most of the Howlin's. Some of the crowd came by to slap me on the back and offer to buy me a drink. Maybelle asked what I was drinking and the next thing I knew it really was closing time. Maybelle, who had hung around to ply us with liquor long after she had run everyone else out, slipped me an envelope, which was a cut of the bar from tonight, a nice gesture she had started. Before her, the other managers simply paid me in drinks and I probably ended up owing them money when the night was over. Of course my cut usually was enough to cover the alcohol I drank and bought for my friends since midnight, but it was still a nice thing for her to do and I gave her a big hug and probably a little too much of a lingering kiss on her neck as I stood to leave. My legs felt strangely rubbery as I made my way to the front door. I let out a wolf howl one last time and promised Maybelle I'd be back next year if she'd have me. She said, "I'll keep the porch light on," as she swatted me out the door and locked it behind me.

Sixth Street was about as close to closed as a person might see it at night. There was an officer standing down at the corner and I managed to walk a straight line, at least my best imitation of straight, towards him and pulled myself up trying to look respectable as I handed him a twenty and my room key. He just looked at me with a cross between 'thank you for admitting your sorry ass state' and 'will you people never grow up?' He whistled and a cab swung around the corner and he handed the cabbie my twenty and instructed him to take me to the Hampton as he shoved my key back in my shirt pocket. I turned and declared him an officer and a gentleman and I saluted him as I fell backwards into the taxi. He poked his head in just before he shoved my feet in and slammed the door and said, "The Howlin' sounded good tonight. You're gettin' better. Now go sleep it off." 'A fan' was my last conscious thought of the evening.

V.

I could hear the phone ringing and knew what I was supposed to do, my body just wasn't responding. It was very dark in the room with only the smallest trace of light creeping in through the curtains and as I groped about the darkness in the room as well as the fog inside my head, I made very little headway. My hand bumped a table and I was able to feel my way up to the lamp switch and get some light into the room. The illumination helped me see, but did little to help me comprehend where I was and what I needed to do next. The ringing had stopped a couple of minutes ago and I sat on the edge of the bed and began putting the pieces together. As the mind fog cleared, I recognized my hotel room and looked over to the other side of the bed to see if anyone had followed me home. They had not. It became clear alcohol had been a major part of the previous evening and its effects were still lingering even now at...I searched for a clock...6:30. So early. No wonder I was groggy.

Considering only five hours ago I was still on Sixth Street, I guess it wasn't so bad. How much had I drunk last night? I remembered starting with beer and progressed to a nice Irish whiskey for the last hour of singing. After the show my friends and I had several rounds as we laughed about the crazy shit that had gone on this year with my car wash being the winner. At some point, someone that sounded like me shouted Tequila, and we debated the merits of reposado, blanco, and anejo, having to taste some of each to compare. After several rounds without a clear winner some idiot that didn't sound like me, suggested that Ouzo was really a man's drink so then the battle between Mexico and Greece took place at the table until we all became casualties. I should have stuck with the Irish. They had perfected the art of making liquor that didn't cause you grief even when you abuse it most of the night. Evidently, they got their grief from other parts of their lives so they had to have some place to take solace. As I gradually put together the source of my discomfort, I held my head and debated starting the day or going back to bed. Even the idea of a full plate of eggs and bacon didn't sound good and actually made me queasy enough to lay back flat on the bed. Was I sure no one was on the other side? The phone rang again as I was reaching out to check the lump under the quilt.

When I answered, it was Margaret Flemming, businesswoman extraordinaire and Shasta school board member. She had been instrumental in helping me survive the carwash last fall and we had been friends since she was my theater arts teacher when I first arrived in Shasta. We also were one-time lovers, one time as in once. I counted her as a friend, but was curious as to why she would be calling me in Austin since we rarely spoke except at board meetings.

"Hey Billy, did I catch at a bad time?" she asked.

"No, actually I was just getting ready to go down to the buffet for eggs and sausage then head over to a presentation I was interested in hearing. " I tried to sound casual and totally in control. I was unsuccessful.

"What? You're fixing to eat breakfast?" She asked with more than a little amusement in her voice.

"Yea, I love breakfast and don't you think I attend meetings when I come to Austin? I'm a highly trained professional you know. " I feigned offense at her attitude.

"Listen Billy, it's six thirty at night. Is your highly trained professional ass so hung over you can't tell night from day? Margaret was outright laughing at me now.

"It's night? I missed the whole day? Okay look, I played the Howlin' down at the club last night and then got in a debate over the merits of Tequila and Ouzo. You can imagine that didn't end well. I saw the clock and thought maybe I had just been asleep a few hours. Sorry, you aren't someone I would lie to; I am not thinking straight," I said in a rather confessional manner.

"You've had a hard year and letting loose is good for all of us at times. However, I need you to get yourself cleaned up and clear-headed. You need to be standing tall, looking sharp in the boardroom at 7:30 in the morning. Can you do that?" she asked.

"Sure, not a problem. What's going on?" I asked more than a little curious.

"We just fired Dan Cochran and we are having a special called meeting in the morning at
7:30 and we need you there. None of this information is public so keep your mouth shut okay?" Margaret was able to sum things up usually with few words and had told me everything I needed to know for the moment.

"Hmmmm. See you in the morning?" was all I could think to say as she gave a hurried goodbye and hung up. Funny how clear my head had become and I probably wouldn't have any trouble driving back to Shasta tonight on the adrenaline that was shooting through my veins. I trooped into the shower and turned it full cold until I thought my head would crack from the freezing water and then gradually warmed it up so I could cleanse my self of the evils of last night. I should be well rested if nothing else.

VI.

I strolled into the Shasta High School office door and gave Ms. Shelly a cheerful hello. There were a couple of the teachers standing around that couldn't wait until the school year was over, then couldn't seem to leave for the summer. I nodded to them as I breezed into my office. Ms. Shelly followed as I went.

"Billy, what happened, you aren't due back until next Monday. Is everything alright?" she asked with a level of concern.

"Ms. Shelly, I am here to take you to lunch. We are closing the office for the rest of the day so shoo those folks out and turn out the lights." I directed as I threw a few papers onto my desk and dropped my tie and sports coat over the back of a chair in the corner.

Shelly had been following my movements while standing stock still, "Billy, you know its only 10 o'clock. That's way too early for lunch and we can't just close the office. Are you sure you are all right? You weren't arrested were you? You promised."

I looked up from rolling up the cuffs on my only white shirt and smiled, "Is that Mexican food place downtown Fort Worth still your favorite restaurant?"

"Sure. Best enchilada plate I have ever had and their chile rellenos, well there's just none better. Why?" I had almost lost her to the thought of food, but she gathered herself to ask.

"Because, Ms. Shelly, that is where we are having lunch, which is why we need to leave now, which is why you need to shoo those jokers out there away and lock up the office. We have a reservation!" I kissed her on the cheek as she still was trying to comprehend what had possessed me and why I was acting so out of character.

When I came out of my office a few minutes later after rummaging through my filing cabinet, Ms. Shelly had the lights out, the people gone, and her purse slung over her arm and was standing by the door with a smile on her face.

"I don't know what you are up to," she said as we walked to my pick up, "but I think I like it. It's exciting. You sure it's okay to close the office, right?" Shelly had a hard time not being perfect or shirking responsibility. She wanted to be bad just a little, but couldn't quite let go. I had been working on loosening her up while she had been trying to get me to focus and behave. Maybe we could meet in the middle one of these days.

145

I turned onto the highway, which led into Fort Worth and set the cruise. I was as happy as I could remember being in forever. Shelly had pulled a CD from her purse and we rode south listening to a Reba McEntire's *The Last One to Know.* I wondered if she was sending me a message or asking me a question. All I knew was she had her sunglasses on, a smile on her face, and was humming happily along with Reba. I believe she felt like Bonnie and Clyde and would savor it for a while until the guilt drug her back to Earth. Hopefully, by then I would have made her forget she was skipping school.

"I have waited patiently during the drive, until we ordered, and through one basket of chips and salsa, so what is all this about?" She asked with a look that said enough of the games. It's time to come clean.

"They fired Super Dan on Tuesday. It seems the last time he had gone to Austin in May, he had been arrested for indecent exposure. The police had found him and a stripper named DarLynn skinny dipping in the fountain by the Capital building." I began filling her in.

"Oh my." Was all she said before Miguel our waiter set the enchilada plates before us with a warning the plates were hot.

Once Miguel had refilled our glasses of water and brought more chips and salsa, I assured him everything was great. We ate a couple of bites before Shelly asked. "So how did this just now come about?"

"It seems that once Dan was arrested he called LT to come bail him out. Since Lawrence T. Higgins III is a lawyer and also his buddy, LT managed to get the charges reduced to disorderly conduct so it didn't sound so bad. He also used lawyer client privilege to not inform the rest of the board about Dan's problems even though LT's the board president.

Had it not been for a reporter at the Star Telegram doing some investigative work on school finance issues, this might have blown over. However, when the reporter was checking some background on his story, he came across an arrest record and recognized Dan's name. Since Dan had won a state championship in football and been superintendent in Shasta for thirty years, he's fairly well known in the area. He called a friend in Austin's police force and found out the real facts. The reporter then called Dan and LT for comments, but neither returned his calls, so he made another call to Dan's house and left a voice mail with very specific details and questions related to his arrest."

When I said that Shelly's eyes lit up and a smile started creeping across her face. She even stopped with a fork full of refried beans halfway to her mouth.

"Yep. You guessed it. Thelma heard it and hit the ceiling. With the help of Elmira Johnson, she took all of Dan's belongings and threw them out on the lawn. She called LT and cursed him a blue streak for hiding this from her and threatened to expose them all. LT managed to calm her down long enough to buy time to fix it. She and LT agreed Dan would take the blame and leave town, which would be best for all those involved, and Thelma could play the role of long suffering victim. So LT called the board together on Tuesday afternoon where Dan was fired.

LT had acted offended by Dan's actions and was completely surprised at his behavior. He made a long speech about morals and how each of them were role models for the children of this district, which is why there could be no forgiving Dan. He was sorely disappointed, but Dan had to go. Once the board voted and Dan agreed to sign a resignation letter without arguing or offering comment in exchange for a tidy sum of hush money, Margaret showed LT a picture that had been mailed to her anonymously of him and a stripper. She reminded him of his most recent words about being role models, let him know they were aware he had hidden Super Dan's dalliances, and with the picture, the pressure from Margaret and Dickey Sizemore, another very powerful board member, was enough to convince LT to step down and never run for office again in exchange for keeping his involvement out of the public eye."

We sat silently for a while enjoying the enchiladas and rellenos. Mostly lost in thought and savoring the time together, Shelly broke the silence by asking, "So how is Dan. What do you think this will do to him?"

"Funny you should ask," I said. "I saw him this morning down at Mayfield's Steakhouse and Cantina when I stopped to get a cup of coffee and some eggs after driving in from Austin. He came over to my table and visited for ten or fifteen minutes."

"Seriously?" Shelly asked,

"Happiest guy I have seen in years!" I said.

"No way!" Shelly said surprised.

"I'm serious. He came in, slapped me on the back and sat down. Said he enjoyed working with me the last twelve years and although we might not have always agreed, he liked me, and wished me the best. I asked what his plans were and he said he had a place in Arkansas for fishing and over the last several years had been spending more time there. He'd already moved most of his personal stuff since Thelma and Elmira spent most days and night together in or around his house if they weren't at the liquor store or casino. Seems he had grown tired of going home and honestly couldn't wait to get out of town. He flipped me the keys to his office and asked me to turn them in. He said he was headed to Arkansas by way of Austin to pick up a waitress he knew there on Sixth Street. Funniest part was he had gone by his house and picked up a couple pair of socks and a change of underwear off the lawn, but left the rest. He wasn't going to need the suits or ties he said and suggested I go by and get me a few ties in case I needed them. So I did. I picked a few of the basic colors and left most of the ones that was a little out dated. Who would have thought? Dan left laughing loud enough I heard him as he turned the corner on Jefferson heading south!"

We both smiled and ate until we had cleared our plates of every morsel. Shelly was a country girl that wasn't afraid of curves or padding. In fact, she wore her shape well and she was well shaped. When it came to food, she liked to eat and there was none of this salad and finger food for her. She had grown up knowing the value of a good meal and she made me proud every time we sat down to eat. I loved how she ate, I loved how she looked, and I loved how she felt when I hugged her close. I knew all that as I sat watching as she folded her napkin on the table and squared up the dishes for the waiter. We decided since today was turning out to be a special day we would have a sopaipillas for dessert with a little honey and butter.

While Miguel cleared our plates and we waited on the sopaipillas, there was a sense of contentment until a question arose in her eyes and she asked, "So with all this change, does any of it affect you?"

"I was kind of wondering when you might get to that, because yes it does affect me. A lot as a matter of fact," I said.

"Oh no, tell me they didn't fire you, too! Is that what this day off is all about? You don't have a job so we're gallivanting around Fort Worth?" her demeanor seemed to bounce between contentment, surprise, and a then a little concern.

"Now Shelly, I know I have disappointed you at times with my behavior and I realize I could be more mature, but I promise I wouldn't do anything to hurt you like getting myself fired or getting you fired for leaving the office. You have to give me at least that much credit," I said with a little hurt in my voice. Some was feigned and some real.

"Okay, maybe I was a little harsh, it's just there's so much happening right now and like Reba said, I feel like I'm the last one to know! Just tell me what is going on, please," she stated in a way that was heartfelt and pleading.

Just as I took a deep breath to start, Miguel showed up with hot sopaipillas, honey, and butter. Once again I assured him all was great and off he went.

I knew Shelly wasn't eating a bite until I finished so I jumped in. "I met with the board this morning at 8 o'clock and they asked me to be the new superintendent."

"Seriously. After all the hell most of them have given you over the years? Now they want you to run the district?" she asked.

"Yep," I said. "It helps that LT was sent packing and it appears Margaret will be the new president. Dickey has promised his support and over the course of the next few months there will be a couple of replacement board members that will be picked that care about the kids and not politics. So it seems there is a new attitude and finally Shasta schools might have a chance to flourish under the right kind of direction and the board thinks I am the man for that job. "

"So did you take it?" She asked now leaning towards excitement.

"I told them I would let them know this afternoon," I said reaching for a sopaipilla. "I needed to think about it."

"What's to think about? You would be great and finally everyone would have a person that understands." Shelly was getting pretty wound up by now.

"I needed to talk to you first." I put down the buttered sopaipilla.

"What do I have to do with this? I think its great. Go for it," she emphasized waving a butter knife.

"Look, we've been together for twelve years and I couldn't have made it without you. You have kept me together and given me a reason to get up every morning. I can't do the superintendent's job without you and I needed to know if you'll be there." As I talked she softened.

"Are you asking me to move to Central with you? To take Gladys Newman spot as superintendent's secretary? I can do that. Sure. No problem. We make a good team," she finished as if all was solved.

"No. I'm not asking you to be my secretary," I slid the box that I had rummaged around in my filing cabinet to find, across the table. In it was a diamond ring. "I'm asking you to marry me. I've known a long time you are the best thing to ever happen to me, but I have been waiting until I matured a little so I could offer you the life you deserve. It seems as though I won't ever completely grow up, but at least I now have a respectable job and can make you a respectable husband. So Shelly Connors Smitherman Wharton, will you marry me and make me the happiest man alive?" I asked, having slid out of my chair and on as close to bended knee as I could get with my bad knees.

I really think I surprised her. Very few times has Shelly been caught off guard or not been in control. This might have been the first and last time, but for the moment she was stunned. And then I began to panic. What if she said no? Did I just mess up the best thing I had going for me? All kinds of crazy thoughts worked their way through my head until I saw a tear run down her cheek and she smiled as she took the ring. As she slid it on her finger she nodded her head and started to speak.

Miguel dropped in one last time to see if we needed anything else and to just drop off the check, which he would take care of when we were ready. I thanked him, praised his service and promised to ask for him the next time I came in. As he bustled away, I turned back to Shelly who had used the interruption to regain her composure and wipe her eyes.

"Billy, I would love to marry you," she said in a much more controlled voice. "I wasn't sure you were ever going to ask. When were you thinking we might get married?"

"If I take the job, I start July 1. That gives us a little over two weeks for a honeymoon. What do you say? Beach? Mountains? Cruise?"

Once again she paused and I saw just a little mischief creep into her eyes. "They say all ceiling tiles look the same so I guess it doesn't matter. Just make sure I can get enchiladas at least once a day with a margarita on the side." I could smell the Pacific Ocean already.

I slid a couple of $20's on the table as we left arm in arm. Who said the wedding had to be before the honeymoon?

Rolling Final Credits

Well that's my story, at least as best as I can remember it. I never lie about anything other than the size of my manhood or the size of fish I caught so this had to be my life up to now. Unless, of course, I misremembered a few details that probably weren't that important anyway. My friends have been good friends and well my enemies, as you can see weren't really that much of an enemy after all. I guess in the heat of the moment things take on a whole different dimension and we have a tendency to blow things out of proportion. The good news, looking back, it was never as bad as it seemed and a lot of times it was kind of funny. I still laugh thinking back about Abigail Fisher's face when I thanked her for appraising my prick to be a winner. Had we been in a cartoon, her head would have exploded right then and there.

I look back at my journey across more than a few school districts in Texas and feel blessed having known some really good teachers and of course the kids. I always wonder how they'll turn out. Fortunately, I have been at this long enough to be able to see their names in the paper as they accomplish this or that and thankfully only occasionally do I see names I know in the police arrest report. I introduced you to a number of folks along the way and you can probably imagine how their lives turned out. It's good for the creative juices to develop you own story lines and wonder how close you might actually be. If you like that sort of thing then knock yourself out.... but if you are the kind that doesn't like loose ends and really love those movies where they tell you what happened to the main characters as they roll the final credits, then turn the page and I'll share with you what I think happened and see if you agree.

Boomer

Boomer was the natural choice to take over as high school principal when I moved up to the main office. He had learned about as much as I could teach him and knew the kids and school as well as anyone. I knew he was going to be okay when the first thing he did was go out and hire a little five foot nothing spitfire by the name of Penny Ball. Everyone called her Pinball because she never stopped moving and appeared out of nowhere. Some suggested Dodge ball would be better because most people heard her high heels clicking and they dodged into a doorway or closet. She never seemed to tire and always had an idea how to help make things better. They were good ideas too; they just required some effort on people's part.

Boomer had followed one of my ten commandments, which was focus on your strength and hire to your weakness. He knew there wouldn't be any discipline problems with him in charge and he could handle the nuts and bolts part of school. What he needed was someone that could work with the teachers and help them to work together when it came to designing lessons and teaching kids. Penny's personality made her popular among the faculty and staff even if they sometimes wished they had heard her coming a little sooner. With the balance of Boomer and Penny, Shasta High continued to improve academically and developed into an outstanding high school.

Boomer did surprise me with one of his moves. He had found himself single as well, after too many nights spent watching film. It seemed he had taken a liking to Donna Clinton over the years as he worked with her to get her kids to school and when I moved her into the office, well it was like putting candy in front of a kid. He and Donna began seeing each other on the sly, and did a super job of keeping the secret. By the time Boomer's first graduation rolled around, he was ready to make Donna a June bride. She even wore white. She considered herself a new woman and I applauded her for the choice. Boomer was really good for Dolan, Donna son that was fixing to be a junior and had turned into an outstanding athlete. With Boomer working with him at home, and he finally having a dad, Dolan made All-State in Football and won a gold medal two years in a row throwing the discus in Austin. Dora was happy for her mom and cried when she was asked to be maid of honor.

Dora chose pre med and wound up graduating in the top five percent of her class. She had a couple of choices for medical school and excelled there as well. Last I heard she was trying to decide on surgery on working in a free clinic.

Super Dan

Super Dan did indeed stop by Austin and pick up DarLynn before they roared off to Arkansas where he spent the happiest two weeks of his life. DarLynn and he ran naked in the woods and even the poison ivy didn't slow them down for long. DarLynn started getting restless though about halfway through June. She liked the bright lights and the big city and honestly all the trees and crickets kind of freaked her out.

After a month, Dan drove her to the bus station in town and bought her a one-way ticket back to Austin. She kissed him long and hard on the lips and left a big red smudge as she boarded the bus and waved goodbye. Dan smiled all the way back to the cabin. DarLynn was fun, but to be honest he was exhausted. He had worked too hard all his life to have to work at keeping up with a girl only a third his age. She had almost given him a heart attack on more than one occasion and her needs were getting in the way of his fishing. His needs right now were to be able to doze in the boat when the fish weren't biting and to be able to doze in his chair when the ball game was on. Other than that, well if he needed it, he'd worry about it at the time. I guess he's still there...dozing.

Thelma

Craziest thing. Thelma and Elmira Johnson were coming back from the liquor store over in Muenster one afternoon and got pulled over by the highway patrol for speeding. They had been in a hurry to get back to the DAR club meeting on time so no one would notice they had slipped out of town during the day to resupply their liquor cabinet. Elmira had moved in full time once Thelma had thrown Dan's stuff out on the lawn and it took a lot of liquor for the both of them.

When the officer looked in the back seat he saw four cases of liquor, two cases of gin, and one each of vodka and rum. He arrested them both for bootlegging. The arrest was news, but the trial...well it made national headlines. The defense attorney had made a video of him deposing them in front of the county prosecutor. He asked them questions and to perform physical activities over the course of several hours. All during this time they each were sucking down gin straight from a bottle. At no time did either one of them show the slightest effect from the large amount of alcohol in their system. Finally, having watched about half an hour of the video and having the prosecutor admit that even in the end, no change occurred in their behavior, and that he himself had verified it truly was gin, the judge threw the case out. He acknowledged they could indeed drink that much liquor themselves and had no intention of selling it to under age boys. He did suggest they get some help to which they scoffed and marched out.

The unusual defense kept Thelma out of jail, but it eroded her standing in the community and the pastor at First Baptist suggested she step down from her role as head of the ladies auxiliary. From there it was one club after another asking her to resign until her and Elmira decided to sell the house and move. They needed a new start and Shasta held nothing but bad memories. Last anyone heard they were living in Taos and had some medicinal plants growing in the backyard to help with their alcohol withdrawal. They didn't try to withdraw from gambling and not too far down the road was an Indian casino that kept them happy. They tried to watch the sunset each evening.

Coach Debbie Connelly

Debbie and Demarcus Latham got married after the school year ended and he did ask her to move to the home he had built in Florida. It had an infinity pool just as I imagined. She played some beach volleyball for a while, but then it turned out she was pregnant. She gave birth to a son that had somehow been blessed with the best genes of each of his parents. He would grow up to be almost seven foot tall with the build of defensive lineman, but the agility and grace of his mother. He would excel in basketball like no one else had before him. After leading his team to its third straight NBA title, he retired and moved to Hollywood to make movies. He still calls his mom each week to check on her.

Sylvia Benson

One of the first meetings I had after being named superintendent was with Sylvia. She was dressed for success and ready to get down to business with a new boss. I could see most of her packaged goods from about any angle as she crossed and uncrossed her legs and leaned in close to make a point. I closed the door after a few minutes of lighthearted discussion about the weather and the town in general, which brought a smile to her face thinking she would be able to make some points with me now she was sure.

I leveled with Sylvia about how I felt she was out of her depth and had to rely on her 'personality' to stay afloat. I did compliment her on her ability to do so and how much time she spent trying to keep from being exposed, which seemed ironic in the sensé she had to expose herself to accomplish that. She simply laughed at first and leaned in to give me a better view thinking I must not have gotten a good enough look, but I insisted she had talent way beyond her physical appearance if she would just refocus her efforts. I promised her a chance to learn her job and practice as a director in the district if she would actually learn her craft.

When she realized I wasn't taking the bait or being willing to enjoy her charms while allowing her to continue hosting the district parties and just looking good, she kind of stiffened and for a fleeting second I saw fear in her eyes. Realizing she had some hard choices to make, I asked if she'd like a day or two to think about it and she agreed to get back with me. She thought she might like to actually learn her job and feel good about her role in the district.

I felt good about the possibilities when she left, but wasn't surprised two days later when she came in and turned in her resignation. She thanked me for my candid discussion with her and said I probably knew her better than most and appreciated the fact I thought she had some brains to go along with her looks. She just felt like at this time, as far as she had come, it was too late and too much work to start over having to learn stuff. She had a friend down at the coast that was looking for a special advisor to the superintendent's office and she would be the perfect fit. The pay was good, the hours were flexible, and it was close enough to the beach she could work on her tan after she'd finished advising for the day.

I wished her well and just for old times sake she gave me the old double handclasp and leaned in close. You had to hand it to Sylvia. Talent comes in many different forms and she had talent. I wasn't going to pass up her last show so I took my farewell peek and thanked her. Last I heard Sylvia was back in New Jersey hiding from the superintendent's wife that caught Sylvia advising her husband at home while the wife had been away for the weekend. The husband was able to recover from the gunshot wound suffered during the "accidental discharge" long enough not to press charges and then resign his position. Sylvia escaped during the confusion and caught the first plane north to New Jersey where guns weren't so prevalent.

Joe Bob and Chastity Gordon

For Joe Bob and Chastity going to college in Arkansas was perfect. They could spend time together and feel free to walk in the open holding hands. They loved their classes and joined a church after about the third week when they began to relax. They had no intention of going home, but did visit with their families, separately by phone, and the Internet.

Then, the baby came. Hiding out and pretending was fine for them, but they realized that they had two grandmothers back home that didn't know there was a new grandbaby girl. They considered the options and decided that they had no choice, but to notify the families. That didn't mean that they had to do it face to face. They could see how that might get ugly in so many ways.

They took a picture of sweet little Ashley, wrote out the full explanation about their marriage, how happy they were together, and made the parents aware that they were welcome to visit, if they chose to come in peace. They stuck the letters in the mail and waited...and waited. After the third week, they decided that they had been disowned, so they went on about their business, promising to raise Ashley in a loving home without prejudice. They hated that she wouldn't have grandparents or uncles and aunts, but if they were all hateful, wasn't it better not to know them? They vowed to start brand new, and Ashley would be the first of a new generation.

They learned through their church about an opening for house parents at an orphanage in Pine Bluff. After considerable thought, they decided that was their calling and moved to become foster parents for the kids that needed someone to love them. Over the years, Ashley had dozens of brothers and sisters that would remain close for her lifetime. Joe Bob and Chastity told her about her past when she was old enough and gave her the option of going back to meet her blood relatives. She opted not to.

Ms. Perkins

Ms. Perkins was my friend you met last fall that like to call pretty much on a daily basis to let me know what I was doing wrong or what needed fixing around the school. Living with a houseful of cats left her plenty of time to think after getting off work down at the tax office. When she heard I had been made superintendent she was delighted. Now we could visit about the entire district. She was so excited she got up a half hour early to get her coffee and donut and drive around each campus before work each morning to 'evaluate' the situation.

I finally decided if you couldn't beat them then join them. I hired Ms. Perkins part time and her sole job was to call in a report each morning to a voice mail box and file her report. I made it a point to call her about once a week to update her on how we had handled the issues she had spotted. She had never been happier and honestly there were a couple of times she caught things we missed and I finally gave her a certificate at a board meeting for her diligence.

She came in one morning with a very distressed look on her face and was sad to tell me she had to resign. It seemed she needed to go back home to Victoria and help run the ranch since her folks were getting on in years. She broke down in tears as she apologized for letting me down. I had to say I actually felt bad at that moment for the many times I had cursed that woman. I gave her a big hug and told her honestly the district would not be the same. Last I heard she and her cats were riding heard on about a thousand head of cattle.

Candi Carson

Candi was my former student that had made her fortune working at Hooters. She was blessed with many attributes and used them all to be successful. She had worked her way through TCU, a private college, and then law school with the tip money she earned. I once figured up what that amount had to be for her to pay cash for her tuition and books and knew she was getting paid a hell of lot more than me. But then she had more to offer.

When I wandered into her Hooters in Fort Worth to watch Monday night football several years ago, we recognized each other and I spent most Monday nights at her table during the season eating wings and talking about her and she talked about Shasta. She was smart and I knew she would do great things and she had. She decided one of the key issues in Texas was education so she specialized in educational law. I hired her and her firm as the Shasta ISD legal counsel. She saved my butt more than once and never let us down.

She ran for state senate to represent her district in Fort Worth, which was mainly made up of minorities and won handily. She was constantly in the news railing against the current governor and his good old boy tactics. She was relentless in her attacks on his lack of focus on education for all kids rich or poor. She hammered away at him constantly for spending most of his time with rich lobbyist debating a run for the presidency. Last I heard she had organized a campaign team and had planned to run for governor herself. I will be voting for her if for no other reason than I trust her and she would actually care.

Lawrence T Higgins III

Folks learned a lot about old LT III when he finally got himself in a bind. It seemed his power and money came from his wife's side of the family. His name was well known, but the money on his side had dried up when the Hunt brothers had tried to corner the silver market and sucked his daddy into the scheme. Hunts can come out of something like that still firing, but LT II lost his whole wad along with his ranch, which was leverage in the deal.

LT III had been fortunate to catch the eye of a very wealthy oilman's daughter and managed to sweep her off her feet and into marriage before she truly understood his financial standing. She was a little upset at first, but then realized she had a lot of power with the way things turned out and decide to enjoy it. She let LT parade around and swing his weight to gain control of most businesses in Shasta. She didn't interfere when he took over the school board and ran it like his own company for twenty odd years. Most of the time she was in New York City or Paris looking at fashions or visiting their kids Jennie and Quattro who went to private school in Switzerland.

Mrs. Higgins III didn't ask questions when he suddenly resigned from the school board and pull out of the Mayor's race. She figured it was some kind of political intrigue that she could care less about. When the Securities and Exchange Commission showed up threatening to freeze his assets, her money, unless he cooperated, she asked questions. It turned out LT had been using some insider information to get a large share of stock in a couple of wind power energy companies.

Mrs. Higgins sat LT down and showed him the deal. It was a fairly large settlement of funds that would be waiting for him when he got out of Federal Prison. In exchange for her years of patience and generosity, he would take all the blame, protect her money he had been spending, and move his personal belongs somewhere other than the house they were standing in. If he failed to comply, she assured him he would be in state prison with real criminals and the only thing waiting for him when he got out would be a suitcase full of his clothes left in a room at a boarding house downtown.

Being the smart man he was, he signed, sang like a canary to the Feds, did his time and then disappeared from the face of the Earth. He had cost some very wealthy businessmen a lot of money and a couple of them had spent time in jail along with him. They were not happy and they knew people who knew people that hurt people for a living and those people were after LT. Last I heard, someone thought they saw him in Belize working when they were down there zip lining across the top of the jungle. He looked a lot different, but they were pretty sure

161

he was the one that served them a drink from the cabana bar at their hotel. Then again someone said he was swimming with the fishes off the coast of New Jersey. Either way he was close to the ocean.

Margaret Flemming/ Dickey Sizemore

Margaret and I stayed friends the rest of my time in Shasta. We worked closely together to make a good school. She served as president of the board for another twenty years and when her business interests brought in three new corporations and a lot of employees, we had to build a new school. With a lot of effort, a bond issue was passed and old Shasta High passed into history. It remained a museum and was kept up by the local historical society, which pleased me greatly. The worse thing I had seen was when districts abandoned schools and left them to rot right in the middle of the neighborhoods of the people that had attended them, monuments to the ineptness of the leadership at the time. This wouldn't happen to the old SHS at least not for a while.

Margaret would go on to be elected mayor and drag Shasta out of the last century kicking and screaming into the future. She created a new downtown area, which combined the historical side of the town with modern stores and features. She finally put Shasta on the map. The moment that the people were ready to crown her Queen Mother was the day she snipped the ribbon on our own new Wal-Mart store. Take that Decatur.

Dickey made and lost at least three more fortunes over time, but always had Margaret's back. He continued to be diligent when spending school money, another irony considering how he spent his own. A few years ago when things got bad again and the bank picked up the latest pink Cadillac that the missus had been driving, she decided it was time to get off the rollercoaster. It was fun for a while, but feast or famine had its drawbacks and she was ready for some plain old vanilla average. I heard she caught a bus back to Midland and worked in a fitness gym as a receptionist. Dickey isn't one to give up and the last I heard, he had gotten in on a deal in Brazil where they had just hit one of the largest fields of oil on Earth. I saw a picture in Newsweek during Carnival and I swear that was Dickey doing the Rumba in a parade.

Abigail and Layton Fisher

With Thelma, her aunt, leaving town, any influence she might have had was gone. She became nothing more than another harping drone that soon realized everyone in town avoided her. When she came home one day to find her husband had moved his stuff to the back of the flower store, she decided it was time to leave. Last I heard she was out in Taos close to Aunt Thelma where she had somebody to talk to. Seemed none of the folks there like her either.

Layton? Well he had a love for fashion and managed to start his own line of clothing after coming in second during his appearance on Project Runway. He focused on rugged clothing for outdoor wear and made millions from manly men across the country including his grandpa. Super Dan loved the dungarees with elastic waistbands and the vented shirts, and had been so thrilled to be asked by Layton for his expert opinion on some of the newer lines coming out, that he cried. Layton pretended not to see.

Layton and Dan went fishing twice a year.

Kelsey and Kneisha

As expected, both girls did well in college. Kelsey transferred to the University of North Texas after the first year in Wichita Falls when she decided to focus on music. She graduated with honors, married a young man from Tyler, and had three children. She spent her time singing in the church and was still thinking about recording an album of original music she had written over the years. Most of her inspiration came in the wee hours of the morning as she rocked her babies back to sleep after needing a midnight snack. With her kids almost grown she figured it was about time. Until then she would keep working on the children's book series she had started.

Kneisha finished up at Midwestern setting records in most of the categories available for a volleyball player. She served as student body president her senior year as well. When she graduated, I hired her to come back to Shasta and guide our girls program, which fell off some after Debbie Connelly left. She had done an incredible job, which of course didn't surprise me. She had been running the high school since she was a student there.

The girls in her program came out with fundamentals and a sense of worth. She also taught them character and how to behave. More than once she has jumped on one of her girls for hanging around with some guy she thought was trouble. She didn't mince her words either. Pregnancy rates among students at Shasta High had dipped considerably since she had been back. I gave her all the credit. Guys weren't happy about her 'put a ring on it' policy, but the girls followed her like she was a prophet. I suspect Kneisha had as big an influence on Shasta High and the town as just about anyone I knew and I included myself in that group. It's fun to see someone as they grow and watch as they impact others. Kneisha had it going on for a long time and she didn't disappoint.

Tommy Lucas

I was watching *CNN* a few years ago and they had a story running about the unfair hiring practices or something concerning Wal-Mart. The lawyer for the defendants was a young man by the name of Thomas J. Lucas. He had longish hair and a scraggily looking beard, but was very articulate and spoke with passion. I did a *Google* search and I was about ninety-nine percent sure that this was my Tommy Lucas. His age and graduation dates matched up and he resembled the scared kid that I last saw at prom. His bio showed college and then law school back east before joining the ACLU. I smiled to think that he had been heading for this career his whole life. He needed a cause and didn't ever have one that was his own, but now he could fight on behalf of others for a living. He was a crusader for equality and justice. If we just spent a little more time looking, we could see the promise in all kids. It's there, no doubt. I needed to remember to tell Boomer. He would laugh, I was sure. Surely, by now. Don't you think?

Francie Murdoch

I don't really know what happened to Francie. Her boys never came back for the fall. But I did read that Big Sugar was found guilty of a lesser charge and released for time served. I can only hope they found a place to settle down and put the boys back in school.

Occasionally, when my mind wandered or I heard a motorcycle engine, I could conjure up the image of her leg with its Soft Tail and shorts wedged up. Of course, as it drives off into the sunset of my mind, the butterfly appears and flutters away as well.

People like Francie have lots of hills to climb and I usually count my blessings more than once after working with them. The good news is they are usually fighters and are tough enough to make it through. I guess that's one of the attributes a person develops depending on what the circumstances are. I do know as tough as her outer shell was she was soft-hearted and she loved her kids so I suspect they were taken care of as good as she possibly could. Good Night, Francie, wherever you may be.

Floyd Hammershead

Floyd stopped by Central office a couple of days after I moved in just to prove he had a sense a humor I guess. He walked in and asked if he could ring the bell. I didn't have the heart to tell him there were no bells at Central, but I let him bang on the old school bell I had setting out on my desk. It was one of those counter kind you find at the cleaners when the people are back in the back and you need service. He about hammered it through my desk before I laughed nervously and scooped it away from him.

He plopped down in the chair and asked what I though about him running for school board. He felt he had plenty of experience, with all his kids and all, and a desire to make the schools better. He thought we would make a good team being how we had so much experience together. I asked if he would be willing to take off his rubber boots and wear his Sunday white shirt to board meetings. He left pondering that. I guess the answer was no since he never filed. He still remained my friend and had never failed to say at least once a month, "Playing chicken with a pig! I get it". Fortunately it only took about four months for it to makes its way through the thick bone covering his enormous head. He also brings me milk each Monday. I can't complain. We all need people like Floyd that are solid. I don't want to have drinks with him, but I sure don't mind saying hello regularly.

Ms. Shelly and I

We did take a honeymoon a few days after I signed my contract and before all the craziness started. We flew to Puerto Vallarta for seven days and spent most of our waking hours in a lounge chair soaking up the rays in the shade of a palm tree. Our hands were usually holding a glass of some fruity drink that Shelly discovered that tasted a little like coconut, went down like soda pop, and made you incapable of walking after two of them.

Fortunately, we had a waitress that came by regularly and knew to stop when we fell asleep. Looking across the stretch of blue Pacific Ocean or swimming across the pool to cool off was about as much time as we spent on sight seeing since we had a lot of lost time to make up for and we intended to do as much as we could. Sometimes in the afternoon and every night we pretended to be newly weds on our honeymoon and took turns searching out new designs in the ceiling tiles. I bought Shelly enchiladas at least once a day and we started a collection of tequila bottles that would have served as candle holders in every room in our house had we been able to bring them back.

As far as the wedding, well it took place in October on a Friday afternoon in the chapel of the church. Her kids drove in early from school and served as maid of honor and my best man. I had spent a lot of time with her kids and they evidently had been given good reports about me over the years so we had always gotten along. When Shelly told them we were getting married, I think they were as relieved as excited. Neither was happy with their mother living in sin and had been wondering since they were old enough to wonder why I hadn't asked her before now.

It was a good question and one it took me years to answer. I guess I saw Ms. Shelly as someone special and never really felt like I was good enough for her. It had taken awhile and maybe a little growing up for me to realize that we made each other better in some ways and I actually had a few things I could bring to the table. I knew the first thing was that I would be spending enough time with her to make sure she didn't get bored or lonely and would try to be a regular in her church for Sunday School. She would have to move to the married couples class, which I don't think she was that fond of, but would do it for me if I were going to go with her.

Shelly asked to move out to my house, which surprised me since she had done such a great job of fixing hers up, but I carefully brought all her stuff over one weekend. I figured she would have dust ruffles hanging from everything I owned, but the strangest thing happened. She hardly changed a thing. When I finally asked her about it, she said this house was where she had been the happiest for the last twelve years and why would she want to change that now? That made me smile.

We spent a lot of time on the balcony watching the moon come up and just between you and me, we have played chase on more than one occasion running naked through the house with the blinds open. I think she loved the freedom and was glad to have an excuse to not be perfect. It helped she didn't have to work too hard to be better than me.

Funny thing. I figured my howlin' days were over and had pretty much marked that off my list. When I mentioned in passing about sending out a notice about its demise, Shelly got almost irate. She hadn't heard me sing in public and thought that was something that she needed to do at least once. The following June, Shelly and I drove south to make sure there was an eleventh annual howlin', especially since the t-shirts had already been printed. I didn't know if it was having Shelly sitting up front, and at times on the piano bench, that made the night better, or the fact that I was sober and more lucid. Bottom line, we all had a good time, and I felt a heck of lot better waking up in Shelly's arms the following morning over at the Hampton without a headache. My biscuits and gravy tasted better as well. Last I counted, there were twenty-four t-shirts in my drawer. Seemed like a good number since we could howl on our own back porch anytime we felt like it.

I wound up serving as superintendent for a number of years, but nothing even close to Super Dan's record. What I lost in longevity, I made up for in effectiveness and when it was time to pick up my plastic cube with the school crest, I received a standing ovation in the new auditorium of the modern looking Shasta High School. Margaret presented my award to me and shook my hand before we hugged each other for a long time.

Shelly worked right up to the time I decided to retire, not wanting any part of sitting at home or learning how to knit or going to any of those garden clubs. She had been working her whole life and didn't know how not to. She got her plastic cube along with me. I presented hers to her and then we hugged for a long time.

As you can tell I like happy endings. It's not always easy because life has a way of throwing us curves. What I know for a fact is that happiness isn't about stuff so much as it's about the people in your life. If that's the gold standard, I'm a very happy guy.

About the Author

Gene Suttle is retired after 35 years in the Texas Public School System. He was a Teacher, Coach, and Principal during his career while serving in ten schools in seven different school districts across north Texas. During his last 14 years he was principal at four different high schools. As many have, he vowed to write a book about the crazy life of an educator. And now he has...three times.

Gene is married. He and his wife Lisa have two children who are also married and have children of their own. He currently is a full time Papi and part time writer.

Acknowledgements

My wife Lisa and I have shared the High Life for thirty-four years, and, like most couples, it has been eventful, mostly in a positive way. She has been my number one supporter, collaborator, and critic, mostly in a positive way. I thank her for her efforts and input.

I want to thank my classmates from the Hereford High School Class of 1972 for the times we shared together and the overall atmosphere that provided a foundation on which I built my educational philosophy. My goal was for every one of my students to have a positive memory of their high school years like I do. I don't know if I was 100 percent successful, but that was the goal. I'm sure I have blocked out some of the more embarrassing moments and moments of insecurity, but I enjoyed high school enough to keep doing it for another thirty plus years. Thanks guys.

Growing up, I didn't have imaginary friends. I had a football I learned to kick to myself if no one could play. That skill didn't pay off in the long run as I learned during my first Punt, Pass, and Kick contest, but it did keep me entertained. During the summer there was a baseball I could throw onto the roof if the neighbors were gone or busy. During the last few years I have spent more time with the characters in these books than just about anyone else and have grown to like them very much. I have lived their lives inside my head so long that I suspect when that old age memory thing kicks in, I might be discussing these characters as if they were actual friends in the past. I hope if you're the one listening, you'll understand they did play a part in my life and to me they are real.

Made in the USA
Middletown, DE
17 February 2019